The Nightmare Box and Other Stories

Cynthia Gómez

ISBN (paperback): 979-8-9884138-2-0
ISBN (ebook): 979-8-9884138-3-7

Critical Praise for Cynthia Gómez

"*Nightmare Box* is an unflinchingly honest collection packed with full, rich characters. Throughout, Gómez deftly intertwines the historical and the supernatural to craft human stories that are sharp, and precise in their confrontation of structural injustice. She centers the inner lives and isolation of those who are forced into liminal existences while showing us that respite can be found in the most unexpected places. This is a book filled with vital stories that I loved."
-Suzan Palumbo, author of *Skin Thief: Stories and Countess*

"A powerful, and empowering, collection of fantastically terrifying tales centered in Oakland, and the experiences of Latine, Queer and Working-Class people living there. *The Nightmare Box* by Cynthia Gómez is fierce and magical, while confronting very real issues faced by marginalized communities today."
-Cynthia Pelayo, Bram Stoker Award-winning author of *Crime Scene*

"Cynthia Gomez deploys a gift for layering the poetic atop the grotesque, an empathy for seeing a victim forced to be the villain, and the vision to see the horrific in lived experiences. These tales thrum with heart, a livewire pulling readers through the collection. In turns heartbreaking and heartwarming, Nightmare Box signals the arrival of a promising voice and career in horror."
-LP Kindred, writer, editor, podcaster, cocoa-founder of Voodoonauts

"With horrors that start tame only to rapidly grow more vicious and more violent as the suffering of marginalized people continues, Cynthia Gómez's The Nightmare Box and Other Stories is a sharp collage of brown rage that laces queer history with the supernatural to make something unabashedly, radically, Latine."
-Mara Olivas, author of *Sundown in San Ojuela*

"A lyrical, defiant collection. Gripping is right and yet not enough—these characters clutch your face and say 'Don't look away' while staring down you and the world itself. I couldn't tear myself away."
-Hailey Piper, Bram Stoker Award-winning author of *Queen of Teeth*

Contents

Notice of Content Warnings

Content warnings for each story are available in the back of the book.

To the real Manuel, and to his friend, the one who told me Manuel's story. And to the better world that Manuel, and all of us, deserve.

Lips Like Sugar

T he first thing Viviana noticed, on her first night as a vampire, was how much she wanted to fuck everyone. When she was alive she'd been drawn to the same few types, again and again, and she had always longed for a palate more adventurous, more brave. Now everyone she passed smelled wonderful, the hunger sharpening inside her with every breath, and she wanted to slide her mouth over the softness of every neck and take them all in. She felt her skin waking up, beading with cold sweat, a feeling she remembered so well from the beginning of her time with Ravi, her ex. Those day-long hikes on misty trails where desire was so strong it pulled them into hollow trees damp and covered with moss. Everyone she saw now under the streetlights was sending her cold limbs thrumming with the want, like a scarlet nail against a metal guitar string, like a theremin.

Wait, she told herself. *Wait.*

On Friday morning at ten her phone screamed her awake in time to slap concealer under her eyes before her Zoom interview.

(How did vampires get jobs in the old days?) Sheets hung all over the windows of the messy space that belonged to Ravi's friend Sara, who'd heard of the breakup and had kindly offered up her bedroom while she was backpacking to the middle of nowhere. The lamps of the borrowed room burned Vivi's eyes, but faintly, like the after-mark of a sunburn. The interviewer kept looking at her phone.

"Looks like you've had a lot of different jobs. May I ask if you see yourself being a janitor long-term?"

Vivi just nodded, her smile too shallow to show her new baby fangs. *Probably a lot longer than you can imagine.*

"Why did you seek out the night shift?"

Vivi sucked at her teeth, glad the woman's open-necked shirt wasn't within her reach.

"Well, I ... finally accepted that I'm just a night person. I'm at my best when everyone else is sleeping."

"Like a vampire?"

Vivi had to turn her laughter into a cough.

"And the employer's not a problem? All those bodily fluids?"

"Oh, no." Vivi could feel the blood thumping inside her, as if calling for reinforcements.

⁕

Sunday night at nine would be her first shift. Saturday night she walked around Broadway until she found a bar called Este, full of beautiful people, mostly Black and brown, and she let herself sway in the crowd, taking in all the glistening skins and the glorious smells. She let her own skin prickle with the want if someone brushed against her, but she touched none of them back, these people who almost surely woke up in the daylight. Instead she fixed her eyes on the janitor, a short and thick woman a few years younger than Vivi, with faded tattoos on her neck and breath of sweet mint when she told Vivi where the bathrooms were. Vivi let the intoxication spread her lips into a hot grin, and as if in response she saw a flush descend from the girl's cheeks down to her throat. Less than ten minutes later she was pressing the girl up against the locked door in the janitor's closet, watching the beautiful mouth contort in screams hidden by the thumping bass of Azealia Banks.

When the girl came off work at two a.m. Vivi was waiting, and the girl drove them in her roommate's borrowed car back to Antioch, straight to the girl's bed ("Lisa. My name is Lisa. Please ..." she gasped with Vivi's mouth at the swell of her breasts,) and after they had drifted in and out of sleep several times Lisa's hands slid along the rolls at Vivi's waist.

"You're so hot."

"Thank you." Vivi wished she could blush.

"I mean, yeah, that too. But you're so hot."

———⋅∘⋅———

When Vivi's alarm buzzed her awake, she wanted so badly to stay in that place, the air warm and thick, blackout curtains already protecting against the encroaching dawn. But she kissed Lisa's lush mouth goodbye and walked the two miles to BART.

The dark platform was covered with bodies waiting for the 4:15 train. Vivi's thirst, still unquenched, was now thick on her tongue and pounding in her head. Wait. Wait. At least the hunger was softer now, thanks to Lisa, although her hands still throbbed with the wish to slide over every body she saw, pulling aside the uniforms, from construction worker to train dweller, feeling the rush of their blood under her bones. Before leaving Lisa's room she'd pawed through a dresser and stolen a pair of pink gloves. Now she pulled one off, and just as she'd planned it the scent of Lisa, encased in the wool, rose into the air from Vivi's naked hand. She rode the whole way home caressing her own face, breathing in the incredible scent perfuming the air. No one even blinked.

Sunday night was her first shift at Journey Diagnostics, and her thirst was practically clawing at her throat, every body she passed seeming to pulse with fresh veins. She had to keep her mouth shut against her eager fangs as she greeted her supervisor, Jesús, a hiccup of a man in a pale blue shirt. Jesús eyeballed her and handed her a uniform, an access card, a ring of keys, yammered about safe lifting techniques while walking them right past the rooms where the blood was stored. Finally he opened a door and inside were rows upon rows of workstations, samples being tested, the maroon liquid nearly glowing in the overhead lights.

When he finally left her alone she gripped the cart and rolled it into the emptiest row, eyes on her mop, on the floor, while the blood was tested and then tossed into Biohazard bins. When one of the techs got up for coffee she pushed the cart toward the bin, hard enough to throw it and its contents onto the floor. "Shit!" she said, louder than she needed to, in case anyone could hear, and she knelt down and slid three vials into her bra. She made herself replace the bin on the wall, even though her fingers were grasping for the vials, ready to tear them open and splatter her hands in scarlet that she would have to lick off.

In the narrow bathroom stall she pulled open the first one, and she could smell the danger right away. *You could have told me this stuff yourself, asshole*, she cursed Andre in her head. After he'd turned her, the only thing he'd done to help was getting her the interview here. She'd stolen a phlebotomy textbook to learn about the chemicals used to test blood, including some that might put her to sleep or send her vomiting a maroon puddle onto the tiles. She threw the shining liquid down the toilet. The next one smelled of warm copper, the color a candy-apple red. Her lips closed around the edge of the vial and gulped it in, and she could feel it warming and coating her throat on the way down. She could take her time with the last one, older and duller but rich and sweet all the same, and her eyes in the mirror looked clearer now as she wiped her mouth and got back to mopping the floors.

When her first paycheck came she posted an ad on Facebook (*Do you need a roommate but still want your space? I work nights and I promise I'll stay out of your hair)* that led her to a couple who rented a tiny little house on Peach Street. They both worked graveyard at an airport motel and drove days for Amazon, and for a rent she could just afford she could have their converted laundry room for fifteen blissful hours a day, Dollar Store sheets tacked up over every window, three layers deep. The night she moved in, the couple were putting their record collection on eBay so they could afford the husband's knee surgery. Vivi felt a pang of guilt as she contemplated her new body in the mirror, this thing that had forever shed its expensive maintenance, if Andre's promises could be believed.

At her next paycheck she bought real blackout curtains and treated Lisa to an Uber home from Este, Lisa half asleep and half moaning at the tug of Vivi's lips at her throat. The baby fangs pressed against Lisa's veins, but Vivi reminded herself of her promise, the one she'd actually managed to keep in the days since her turning: Do no harm. She'd been raised by a Mexican grandmother in a house littered with crosses and so by the time she was sixteen she'd been holding back her desires for years. Until the afternoon her grandmother came home early to find Vivi and her girlfriend Nidia making out on the couch and her response was, "I kind of knew that. Baby, you left the bathroom a mess. Go clean it up. Nidia, are you staying for dinner?"

⁕

The nights she didn't go home with Lisa she wandered into dark places where she could sate her hunger, but never her thirst. She was fascinated by the effect her desire had on its objects, the way its power seemed to intoxicate her and them both. There was the barber who blew the last of the hair off her neck and then pulled down the shades and bent her over his green leather chair. The woman in the white sweater and flat shoes who smelled like night-blooming jasmine, who protested, "Aren't I a few decades too old for you?" as Vivi slid aside the damp wool and tasted the woman's neck. Vivi loved the sweet tension of pulling her swelling fangs away from their veins. She loved curbing the strength that she was thrilled to feel pushing through her skin, which in defiance of all myths had remained its same rich brown, except for the black circles under her eyes when her thirst was at its peak. She wondered if it would always feel this exciting, this knowing she could have nearly anyone she wanted, the intoxication that came from walking into places full of strange drunk men and knowing that she was nobody's prey.

One night before work she walked right into a coffee shop and sat across from the kind of man she had never bothered with before, slim and pale and shy, enormous headphones around his ears making him look like a hungry insect. He took her back to his apartment overlooking Beeryland and they ignored his roommates banging on the door for them to quiet down. While she was putting on her uniform she could hear the roommates' dramatic argument, something about Instagram photos and why one of them hadn't proposed yet. She realized how little she missed that life, maybe how little she'd ever wanted it. Memories of when she was alive had begun drifting away fast, but she remembered how unmoored she had always felt from the world. Her roots had been so shallow and thin even after thirty-one years, leaving nothing for anyone to hold onto, not even Ravi, a man who could make anything bloom.

She kissed the shy man goodbye at the door, his blood smelling delicious, and another roommate (how many of them were there, anyway?) looked over her work uniform and laughed: "Who's slumming?" And a desire rose in her from somewhere that was neither hunger nor thirst. She pictured herself pulling the roommate into a bathroom and pushing down his boxers, tongue and teeth landing on the vein pulsing in the thickest part of his thigh. The life leaving his body, his head rolling back. "Do no harm," she whispered, and left that apartment behind, running her tongue over her baby fangs as the elevator took her down. The fangs liked to poke through even at the most inconvenient times, but they would retract if she concentrated hard. She made herself read the elevator repair certificate and the package theft warnings and anything else within sight, and by the time she was back out on the street she looked normal to the outside world, nothing to see.

Back on Peach Street she started to hear whispers from her housemates, rumors that the landlord was planning to sell. Vampires in movies never got eviction notices, never had to worry about packing up those velvet-lined coffins that she was pretty sure were a myth. She slept just fine without one. And of course they were always rich, money always flowing into the cracks of their existence. Like the one between their unchanging faces and the dates on every official document they had, a gap that for Vivi was narrow enough now but would widen every year. Lisa was undocumented; that dark space was where she lived.

At work, there were dangers of a different kind. She could manage on only one vial a shift, but she didn't dare steal more than four at a time, the most that would fit into her bra. There were nights, too many of them, when only one was safe.

Then there was the tiny thread of hallway just outside the bathrooms, where sometimes the thirst would turn her careless, drinking even before she was safely inside. One night she was pulling away the lid of a vial when behind her she heard a cough. It was the shift supervisor, Jesús. She dropped the vial and in the clatter of the plastic onto the floor she could hear all of it: the click of the handcuffs, the cell door locking her in for days or weeks with no relief for her thirst. The sunlight on her skin the first time she had to show up for court, the blisters erupting across her face and her hands. The smile on Jesús' face was thin and wet.

"Did you think you were the only one?"

Relief flooded through her, hot and fast, and the words practically tumbled over each other on their way out of her mouth: "Of course that's what I thought! I haven't met any others yet, just the one who turned me … see, I was lonely after I broke up with my ex and I went on a Tinder date and it was this guy Andre, maybe you've met him? Anyway I convinced Andre to turn me instead of—I mean, you know, of course—and then he did and I then asked him what do I do now but he said he wasn't a fucking tour guide so I've been figuring all this shit out on my own and—"

"Whoa, slow down, sister. You don't need to go telling every-one about your Tinder life. I mean, I might not mind, but we'll get to that. Also, why blood? There's much more of a market for piss, but careful, they watch that real close."

And the flood of relief was cold water now, soaking through her limbs. He handed her the vial and the smile on his face was like the wolf who's told the girl that she'll be in real trouble for wearing that bright red cape, but don't worry, he won't tell a soul.

⸺ ⦿ ⸺

Jesús began showing up in the same hallway as Vivi multiple times a week, his eyes always sweeping over her shirt, no matter how loose she began to wear them. The other women on the night shift warned Vivi away from him, and she noticed the way their voices got higher and weaker as they told her, their eyes suddenly sweeping down to the floor. They showed her the pictures he'd sent them, thumbs blocking out what she shouldn't see. They couldn't tell HR; they needed this job. And when two days later the picture came in from him, the text following, "sure you don't want to help me with this?" she knew she couldn't either. Jesús seemed to have a homing beacon for the women who couldn't afford to speak up. And the next time she saw him he brushed up against her in the hallway and she could feel something against her hip, and when the revulsion and fury drained away, something else poured into its place, like the feeling from the man who laughed at her uniform, but so much stronger that Vivi's fangs pressed against her parted lips. She closed her eyes and envisioned herself lifting Jesús three feet off the floor, his feet dangling uselessly in the air. *Do no harm,* she reminded herself, *and anyway you can't kill your boss and still expect to get your paycheck.*

The days grew shorter and sometimes she spent them with Lisa, the two of them huddling over Vivi's cracked laptop, watching the baking and house hunting and wedding planning shows that Lisa loved and Vivi couldn't stand. Lisa teared up when the happy couple would step out into the lights, frothing gowns gleaming. She loved to draw, big-eyed women in swirling dresses and sparkly shoes, and Vivi noticed that the women in the drawings slowly began to look more like Lisa herself. She liked to pull Lisa in front of the bathroom mirror, with its horrible fluorescent light, and murmur to Lisa how beautiful her skin was, all of it, and she would watch Lisa's spine straighten and her breath come shallow and fast. She would borrow Lisa's phone to look up "fashion design schools" and "online fashion degrees," to make the ads pop up in her absence, planting a seed.

All the same, the cracks were beginning to show, the arguments already repeating themselves. "Why do you *never* want to meet my friends?" Lisa complained when Vivi refused, again, to go play soccer at Jacobsen Park.

"That's not true. I've done stuff with them."

"One time. You went to drinks with us once."

Tell them to stop planning so much shit in the daytime, Vivi knew she couldn't say.

Then there were all the times she left Lisa's apartment in the dark, never staying for breakfast, saying she was in a hurry, that she wasn't hungry. And then there was the freedom Vivi still went out to taste. She kept telling herself she'd stop when it got boring, when she felt done. She hadn't yet.

Even so, Lisa had begun weaving a daydream out loud, of some cute little apartment an easy train ride away from Este, the two of them spending mornings in a tangle of limbs and then going out in the bright of the afternoon to walk their dog, some fluffy little thing Lisa would spoil with kisses. Vivi could feel the truth longing to push itself through her skin. She tried to imagine it, going down on one knee, the way some people might hold out a little box with a ring or maybe a shiny new house key, except that in hers was a vial of blood. And then she would pull Lisa onto her lap: "I have something I have to tell you." Something Lisa wouldn't believe, the way Vivi hadn't believed it herself, not until the pain howled its way through her limbs, turning her skin thirsty and cold.

One night in early December Vivi showed up at Este at closing time as she often did, to find Lisa waiting for her with a bag of Vivi's stuff. "I know you never lied to me. You said you could never promise to only be with me. And I said I was okay with that, but"—she sucked in a breath, making her face passive, this girl who cried at reality shows—"I don't think I am. Not anymore. Do you think we could …"

Vivi closed her eyes, feeling the tears roll over her cold cheeks. Here was Lisa summoning all her courage to ask for what she needed, even if the answer was "no." Vivi had known that the end had to come sometime, that someday the cracks would be too wide for either of them to reach across. And here it was, come way too soon. Too soon for that little vial, to ask Lisa to give up every sunrise for the rest of her days. And hadn't Vivi done so much of this when she was alive? So many promises she'd made to Ravi, to the lovers before him, promises she'd always thought she could keep.

The two of them held each other until Lisa's Uber pulled up, and Vivi walked the seven miles home with the weight of the canvas bag over her shoulder, the bag that Lisa had packed and had ready because she'd kind of known what the answer would be.

Then a week later Lisa showed up at Peach Street without texting, just like in the old movies, and Vivi threw a hoodie over her head and hid her arms inside her sleeves and bit off the gasp as a strip of sun hit her exposed hand. They were diving under the covers before the laundry room door even shut, and she could pretend they were in a safe cocoon, these borrowed sheets in a borrowed bed in a rented house with For Sale signs popping up everywhere along the block. She poured mimosas for them both, tossing her own down the sink when Lisa's back was turned, and then Vivi lay there watching her dream, feeling the pulse of Lisa's blood in her neck, marks in the shape of a mouth on Lisa's throat, like sugar spots on a peach, the room filling with the scent of her, and Vivi had never thrummed more with desire in her life. Or after it.

Two nights later Vivi stood on the Coliseum platform, not shivering in the chill. She needed to sneak in to work a little early, see if she could steal a quick drink. Lisa was sending flurries of texts, none of them touching the distance that still yawned between them, the questions neither of them wanted to ask. Was there a future where that little box might live? Or were they just spooling the end even longer behind them both, making sure it would only bleed harder when the thread finally had to be cut? The images Lisa was sending made Vivi glance over her shoulder, glad she couldn't blush. She started typing: *how many can I give you this time?*

And then the picture crawled across her screen. This wasn't Lisa; this was Jesús, and she could feel the nameless desire stabbing into her ribs, stronger than hunger, stronger than thirst. She let herself imagine the release of finally, finally letting her new fangs serve their use, how sweet her thirst would feel when it was just about to be quenched. She imagined his blood still warm as it coursed into her mouth, and she slid her thumb over the screen of the phone, back and forth. She had plenty of time before she had to clock in. Another text came in: *You sure? No roommates ... I live alone.*

Back in September, when she'd swiped right on Andre's profile ("I like hot nights and cold days") it wasn't only for sex, but also for a night away from a bedroom borrowed from a friend of her ex, the awkwardness of feeling both unwelcome and grateful. It was delicious to see Andre's face when he realized she wasn't afraid of his fangs, but instead saw something she wanted. It wasn't so much the thought of eternity. It was never again wondering how she'd pay for both rent and food in the same month, no more worrying about checkups and fillings and the specter of hospital visits she could never pay for anyway, the cost of maintaining a body that would still get weaker and sicker and old. The ability to finally walk at three a.m. in joyful solitude and without fear. "But I won't become a killer," she'd sworn, half-contorted in pain, begging for Andre to finish the turning.

His laugh was cruel. "That's what I said too. But once you open that door, it's going to want to stay open."

"I mean it," she'd told him, her voice weak and thin. He'd regarded her carefully. "Maybe you do." And then he'd leaned in to finish the job, her blood fresh on his mouth.

The speakers crackled overhead; the train would arrive at 7:09. Jesús was taking her silence for consent and kept sending pictures. *You might want to rethink that,* she wanted to tell him. And then the next picture came in, and she could tell from the shapes in the window behind him just what building he was texting her from. She'd been in that very building, in fact, on one of her roving nights out, a crumbling thing with dark hallways and a front door that didn't close. She could find his apartment number from a mailbox, a package left in the lobby. He wouldn't know she was coming until she was already there. She could drop her phone on the train floor, no trace to lead back to her. Maybe she'd only warn him, drawing just enough to leave him feeling dizzy and weak. And afraid. "This is what happens when you can't keep it in your pants," she could shout behind her as she slammed his front door.

"Who's gonna believe you?" he liked to say to women when he rubbed up against them in the halls. "Careful with that, Jesús," she told the empty air. "They might not believe you, either." She licked her lips. The train was coming.

A Kiss to Build a Dream on

Eddie knew it was a mistake to have left the drag show without changing his clothes. He'd been distracted, eyes glued on the young man with the lush mouth he'd been eyeing from his barstool while sipping a virgin Mai Tai. He'd felt the name of the drink stain his mouth and cheeks like a blush, as if it were announcing his status to every soul in the bar. Like Eddie, the slim young man was only half watching the show, and then he had finished his Old Fashioned and slipped out the front door.

Eddie had followed, thinking only to watch him from a distance, just for a block or two. The tailored suit was dipping in and out of patches of light from the doorways, neatly camouflaged, ready to step onto a streetcar and blend in with the late-night crowd. Then Eddie glanced down Telegraph, to where it met Broadway, and he saw them: two cops, leaning on a squad car, hatted and bored and looking for just the right kind of target. The young man must have seen them; the linen suit and shiny shoes were gone, headed down 17th.

Eddie felt his blood thump in his veins, felt his silky blouse stuck to him like a pink flag, the bulls practically pawing the ground in front of their car. His light jacket was hanging neatly on a coat rack inside Lola's, and if he went back now he would lead the bulls straight there.

And then there it was, just in time, next to a shuttered bookshop: an arched doorway and a storefront that he could have sworn had been dark when he'd walked by just an hour before, the door swinging open and lights blinking weak and pale. He ducked inside, and a clerk in a flowered headscarf was straightening a display in dusty glass.

"Welcome! What can I find for you?"

"Yes, I need ..." Eddie's voice, the panic beginning to drain away, sounded too loud for this dusty place. This clerk could have fit right in at Lola's, Eddie was sure: The voice hovered somewhere between a man's and a woman's, and those thick eyelashes and rosy lips seemed to point in one direction, while the muscles straining at the arms of the silk shirt were arguing for quite another. The clerk's eyes were a shade of dark gray, like the pavement after a rain, and the light seemed to follow the flowery scarf as the clerk slipped out from behind the counter. The place felt swirly and dim, a narrow space between here and somewhere else.

"A jacket, perhaps?" And the clerk opened a beautiful Art Deco armoire and took out something in rich black cloth, slipping it over Eddie's arms and buttoning it over his thin raspberry blouse, nearly smothering the bright pink. He'd been sure it would be too large for him, but the fit was perfect, like an embrace.

"And now of course a tie ..." Something silky caressed Eddie's neck, the same gray color as those rainy eyes, and now the pink could barely be seen. The clerk smiled and tucked the brightness further behind the gray folds. "Don't worry; it's still there. Glad to help out; is it Mr. ....?"

"Eduardo." Fascinating. Eddie's family were the only ones who called him that, the ones who saw him before he combed his curls into a neat wave and shined his Florsheim shoes to a punishing gloss. But they never saw him when he dusted his eyelids with glimmering powder in tight canisters and brought his pounding heart into places like Lola's, or the Hilltop Bar on MacArthur, where he would glance at beautiful men he couldn't summon up the nerve to approach. Tonight was the closest he'd ever got to anyone, and look where that had led. He felt the stain of his lips, pale tan, aching with having never been kissed.

"You need just one more ... a hat, perhaps?" And there at the clerk's side in the swirly light was a hat tree, tall and tarnished copper, women's and men's styles all jumbled together in a wave of colors, from bright to dim. The second from the top fairly leapt into Eddie's hand, a green deeper than forest and soft as new ferns.

"There. May these serve you well and see you safely home. Hope to see you again, Mr. Eduardo." The door swung open to a tinkle of bells and Eddie was back under the streetlights, tipping the forest-colored hat as he walked past and just caught up to a streetcar. He realized only after the car pulled away that the clerk had never asked for any money.

All that week Eddie found himself opening up the closet where he'd stashed the black jacket, marveling at the skill in its stitching, the sleek fabric finer than anything he'd ever owned. He thought to wear it to dinner with Melinda on Friday, but when he stretched it out on his bed the slippery fabric slid straight to the floor, and he picked it up but it slid directly back. As he held it up again he caught a whiff of a strange smell he hadn't noticed before: a ghost of mildew, despite how pristinely clean he kept his closet. There was no time to air it out; he was already late to meet her, as he usually was.

When he got home that night, good and early—she'd blinked slowly when he said his stubborn headache had returned, and had been utterly silent in the taxi—he found himself standing at the entrance to the closet again, and pulling the sleek cloth from the hanger, this time not a hint of mold. Instead what came through was a faint whiff of bourbon and orange peel—both found in the Old Fashioned that the lovely young man had been sipping—and Eddie pulled the jacket's arms around himself to breathe the richness all the way in.

Eddie's parents both worked swing shifts at the Mother's Cookies factory (no one lacked for sweets in the Murillo household). His cousin Lili was out on a date and his older brother

Tomás had been killed at the Battle of Midway. So there was nobody home to see Eddie's thin fingers start the ancient Victrola, and nobody to see his shining shoes glide across the worn linoleum of the kitchen floor, draped in the arms of the jacket that smelled of the lovely man, while Bessie sang about the sugar she wanted in her bowl.

The doors were quiet for once as he slipped through them, the floorboards calm and mute as his feet rattled the steps. The knot of the tie had almost tied itself, when ties had always vexed his fingers terribly. It puffed up as if in pride at his neck, a fussy, silky little thing; and the jacket hugged his chest, the scent of orange peel in the air, as he ran for the bus that would take him downtown.

He thought to pass by the shop on his way—how had he failed to catch its name?—and see if the dapper clerk would accept any money, but the only arched doorway on the block was shrouded in a metal grate, the windows covered in boards thick with what had to be almost three years' worth of dust: A gap between the boards showed a stack of yellowing newspapers, headlines praising the storming of the beaches at Normandy. Perhaps the store had been one block over? Eddie knew that his nerves could be easily rattled and that sometimes this affected his memory, but he was still unsettled at the lapse. The tie's knot felt tighter as he passed the dark doorway and the feeling did not ebb until he had passed through a set of double doors and down a winding hallway to a back room, and finally through a heavy metal door to Lola's.

Something was different, and it wasn't just the crowd; more women than the last time Eddie had been here (a poster advertised a Drag King show at 9). It might have been the lights catching off the perfectly tied little knot, or the way his jacket seemed to slide open without Eddie's doing, showing off his cranberry blouse. But as he sat at the end of the bar and glanced at the crowd in little sips, a few pairs of eyes glanced back. And instead of dropping his eyes instantly, Eddie found himself holding their gazes for a heartbeat, even two, every one of them spreading a warmth through his chest and up to his throat, warming the fussy knot of the tie. He slipped through the crowd and fed the jukebox a dime, and all three records were the swingy songs he loved: Louis Armstrong, Billie Holiday, the Boswell Sisters.

"I thought I was the only one here who played that old-fashioned stuff."

The voice was low and smooth and right at Eddie's ear, and it belonged to the beautiful young man in a linen suit, that same lush mouth in a smile so beautiful Eddie actually found himself catching his breath. That smile was shy and open, and a tiny bit sly underneath. His eyes, now that Eddie could finally see them up close, were somewhere between hazel and green. The color was arresting against the richness of his brown skin, a shade or two darker than Eddie's.

St. Elizabeth's High had been a long time ago, yet as Eddie stood in front of the linen suit every bit of those seven years slid away, and there was his tongue feeling twisted in a knot the way it had for nearly every day of those four years, and the blood rushed hot to his cheeks.

"I just like them," Eddie stammered, hating the words as they stumbled out of his mouth. What a smooth way to feed a conversation.

But there was that smile again, the young man's graceful hands sliding over the smooth glass surface where the record spun, the piano notes in time with the thumping of Eddie's own heart.

"I love this record. My landlady complains when I play it late at night, but"—and here the young man lowered his voice, leaning in closer to Eddie—"I can sometimes hear her dancing to it in her kitchen."

Eddie imagined the sweet freedom of a room rented from a stranger, and remembered his own solo dance in the kitchen, Bessie Smith singing about steam on her clothes, and the smile that took over his own face was like a dam breaking. In response, the man extended a hand.

"My name is Lawrence, and ... would you like to dance?"

This couldn't be real. Eddie must have stumbled into a dream days before, perhaps when he stepped into the arched doorway and the dimly lit store just inside. Any moment now he would wake up to find himself alone in his narrow bed, his new radio alarm clock waking him in time to spend all day in the City Clerk's office, typing up neat columns of numbers, eating his sandwich on whole wheat, precisely at noon. "My name's Eduardo, but everyone calls me Eddie."

"What shall I call you?"

Oh, yes. A dream was exactly what this was. Eddie could even hear it in the song, as Louis Armstrong crooned about kisses to build a dream on. Well then, let this be a dream, a dream where Eddie extended his hand to a beautiful young man and let the young man pull him into a dance.

It was everything Eddie had ever imagined it would be. The faint smell of sweat coming from Lawrence, the muscles of his back under Eddie's hands, his mouth lush and wet and so close Eddie could feel his warm breath. No more dancing with the empty air, trying to imagine what this moment might be like, the moment he was living right now.

The song was just reaching Eddie's favorite part, the trumpet soaring joyful and high, the drumbeats building in time; but Eddie began to hear murmuring around him, and a few dancing arms dropped to their sides, eyes darting to the back of the room. He turned and a pink-faced, sweaty man pushed his way up to the bar and shouted something into Lola's ear.

Lola sprang into action as if it were a well-practiced ballet. She pushed firmly through the crowd and cut off the juke-box with a yank of the cord. The bartender propped open the swinging doors that led to the hallway and opened a janitor's closet to reveal a door to an alley. The crowd swelled out of the doors, clip-on earrings disappearing into coat pockets, rouge disappearing onto handkerchiefs, jackets buttoning over bright jeweled tones.

"Get home safely! We'll be back together soon," Lola shouted over the noise, which was not the panicked rush Eddie might have imagined; this was hurried but calm, and he wondered that he wasn't more afraid as he buttoned the jacket over his blouse and yanked his forest-green hat off the hook.

Lawrence grabbed Eddie's hand and said into his ear, "Will you be alright?"

Eddie had never been closer to another man in his life. He was tempted to say no, to hold onto Lawrence's hand and follow him out, but he had no idea what might come next. So he only nodded and watched Lawrence step out through the janitor's closet door. Before Lawrence disappeared he turned back and called out to Eddie.

"Come back tomorrow night. Please."

Eddie took the other way out, through the hallway and back out on Telegraph, finding at his elbow two women in matching suits hurriedly slipping on pairs of clip-on earrings and smearing on a layer of green shadow. The cop cars were just turning down the block, sirens still quiet, lights dark, and Eddie offered up his arm to the woman closest to him. Nothing to see here. A nice young couple and their friend out for the evening, perfectly normal. Three or four storefronts down, next to a bookshop closed for the night, Eddie saw an arched doorway, the lights shining bright and clear, and a door that opened wide for the three of them, and a smiling clerk in a shirt of robin's egg blue.

"Good to see you, Mr. Eduardo! And these must be your charming friends. I'm glad to help you once again. I forgot my manners last time. Please, call me Leslie."

Leslie shut the door with a firm click and made sure the shades were pulled thoroughly down before ushering the women to a display of head coverings: cloche and pillbox and bonnet hats, scarves and snoods in bright scarlet and chartreuse, cloth flowers that could be pinned at a collar or clipped to a bun.

"Remember, friends: three articles of clothing each, from anything in this part of the store," Leslie told the two women, ignoring the questions dancing across Eddie's face and instead laying out a display of gloves, layer after layer in a rainbow of colors Eddie had never seen in leather: peacock blue, gleaming plum, a white like the neck of a dove.

"That one." Eddie pointed to the very last pair, black leather fine and shining and impossibly slim. Leslie glanced at the array of colors and said nothing, sliding the pair out from where they hid, snipping a price tag away from the wristband.

"For you, Mr. Eduardo, I will ask $1.05. Young men should save their earnings for worthier things." The silk shirt was a loose fit, but Eddie could still see the muscles under the robin's egg blue, nearly the same shade as Leslie's glittering eyeshadow, impeccably applied.

Eddie slid a bill and a quarter across the counter and waved away the change.

"Do you have a card? I'd love to come back to your shop when I have … more time to browse."

"My hours vary, Mr. Eduardo. I'm sure you understand. But when I am needed, I am always here." Eddie thought to ask further, but he didn't know how to without being rude. Anyway, "not everything needs explaining" was one of his mother's favorite phrases.

All the next day, as Eddie helped his mother with the breakfast dishes, as he and his father repotted an assortment of spearmint and aloe while his mother wrung out the laundry, he was remembering the feel of Lawrence's hands, the joyful swaying as they danced, the gleaming cop cars at the end of the street. When his mother asked him to help fold the laundry that afternoon, he knew something was on her mind; Lili, who'd been staying with them temporarily for nearly four years, was always the one she pestered for this chore.

His mother waited to speak until they were folding the quilts, a simple two-step dance that Eddie secretly loved.

"Liliana told me that you aren't going with Melinda any more." He had sent off his letter to Melinda only that morning—couldn't his cousin have kept it to herself for even a day? He was glad he'd never told Lili where he went at night, to say nothing of last night's almost-raid.

"I had hoped you could tell me yourself."

"I didn't want to worry you, Mother."

The truth was that as long as there was a Melinda, there were fewer questions. She was better as a costume, like a jacket that covered a feminine blouse.

Except perhaps not like it at all.

"I hope I'm not stepping out of turn, but you didn't seem terribly excited about her."

"I'll find someone else." The quilt had patches of little yellow flowers, cheerful in the chill of the afternoon.

"Eduardo, you know that of course I want you to get married. Naturally, I want grandchildren to love." He didn't need to ask her if she was thinking of Tomás. He knew by the dip in her voice, the way the quilt slacked in her hands. When the War Department telegram came she'd collapsed right there in the doorway, as if she'd had no bones at all.

"I've never told you this, but when I was a young woman in El Paso, before I met your father, there was a man everyone expected me to marry. He was kind and honest and he cared for me, but he wasn't the right man for me, no matter how hard I tried to pretend that he was."

Eddie was very glad for the sound of the ice vendor making his way along their street; it gave him an excuse to turn his gaze away from hers.

"When did you realize that you were pretending?" Eddie's eyes stayed on the departing iceman, his hands gripping the quilt.

"There was a night I was getting dressed for dinner with him and I imagined myself dressing up for our wedding, and nothing about it gave me any joy. And you know how much I have always loved to dress up. It's such a fun thing when it's ... when it's for someone we care for." Her eyes met his and for a second he imagined she knew how often he slid her faux pearl earrings out of her jewelry box, always putting them back before she got home. Then she turned back to the quilt, and he could breathe. Surely she didn't know.

"I still have no idea where I got the courage to call it off. He had money, you see, and we needed it. The store was barely breaking even. I was like you; I couldn't stand to let anyone down, and I knew my parents would be very badly disappointed if I didn't marry him. And they were. They didn't answer my letters for years." She slumped down onto their wooden bench, almost as if she had forgotten she was still holding her end of the quilt, the bright little flowers still in Eddie's hands.

"When you and Tomás were born, I swore I would never repeat my parents' mistake. I know I can't protect you from everything"—and Eddie watched her right hand steal up to Tomás' dog tags, which never left her neck—"but know that I am always your mother, no matter whether you give me grandchildren or not."

She set the quilt into the basket with all the rest, and before she turned and carried it into the house she pulled a little envelope out of her apron pocket. She fumbled in a way that was so unlike her, nearly dropping it before she placed it in Eddie's hand. It held a pair of her earrings, her faux pearl clip-ons, the ones he had borrowed so many times. As she squeezed his hands over them, he wished that he could memorize her face in that moment, the warring emotions written across it, so that he might untangle someday what they meant. She patted his shoulder, like she might do for a small child.

"Remember, Eduardo: Pretending doesn't work forever."

Something in Eddie wanted to tell Lawrence all about the conversation with his mother, to determine what she was really trying to say, but when he walked into Lola's that night, Lawrence leaning against the jukebox and holding out to Eddie a single red rose, he forgot all about it.

While Sarah Vaughn and Billie Holiday sang out from the jukebox, Lawrence swung the two of them around the tiny dance floor and Eddie's clumsy tongue could rest and let the deep voice rumble along. Lawrence loved swing music, bourbon, and his job driving the Number 7 streetcar ("it goes from the Berkeley Hills to the snootier Berkeley Hills," Lawrence said with a wry grin.) Eddie didn't ask him about what everyone already knew: that the streetcar lines would be shut down by the end of the year, turned into buses instead. The songs kept growing faster in tempo, like a challenge, and the two of them met every one: Eddie's hands and his mouth might be clumsy and shy, but never his dancing feet. It was after two Cab Calloway songs that Lawrence leaned in, his hand on the small of Eddie's back, to ask if perhaps Eddie was warm, and if they might walk out for some fresh air?

The fog had rolled in while they had been dancing, and Eddie wrapped a scarf around his black jacket and slipped the leather gloves from his pocket.

Then they were standing in front of a little alley, one that Eddie had passed by before without a thought, and Lawrence was pulling them both into it, where it was almost too dark to see the smile take over Lawrence's face as he gently—so gently—ran a single finger over Eddie's cheek, over Eddie's trembling lips.

The alley was flanked with windows, dark and smeared over with dust, nobody inside to look down and see Eddie's eyelashes flutter as Lawrence reached out a hand to encircle his waist, nobody to hear the gasp of joy from Eddie's mouth as the jacket opened for Lawrence's hand and his soft fingers slid aside the olive green of Eddie's blouse, tracing along Eddie's ribcage, his blood rushing as Lawrence pulled him in for a kiss. Nothing, not the clearest water in the world, had ever tasted as sweet and fresh as this. Lawrence's hands reached for Eddie's, those weak things that had never before known what to do, and now Eddie's gloved hand was pressed against Lawrence's beating heart, and the feel of it was hot and electric, and he had never understood in his life how someone could actually do something that was both danger and peace in the same breath, in the same hungry kiss. Until this.

"Awwwww, ain't this disgusting."

The lights slid across their bodies, the headlights of the car neither of them had heard approaching, the cop car pulling into the alley, doors opening wide, blocking their way out. There they were, the bulls: their eyes practically glowing in the dim light, their nostrils wide with anger and disgust.

Lawrence was already pulling away, his arm stretched protectively in front of Eddie's chest, and perhaps this was what so angered the cops, because it was Lawrence that they both swarmed on, pushing him up against the same wall that Eddie only a few seconds before would have called a magical place. The taller cop's fist met Lawrence's mouth, that beautiful mouth, and Eddie's thundering heart knew that his own was next, that to the bulls pawing the ground in front of him every bit of his body, his very self, was a silky flag waving, waiting to be stained in red.

That was when the hat tightened on Eddie's head, and the jacket's buttons opened, all of a piece, freeing up Eddie's racing heart, and Eddie could feel the gloves heat up against his hands, those things that all Eddie's life had been gentle and meek.

Eddie's gloved right hand reached out and pulled the shorter cop off of Lawrence and swung the cop onto the brick wall. The cop's hands were already taut and poised to strike, and so they braced him as he slammed into the dirty brick, and the wall only shredded his pink knuckles, instead of perhaps snapping them, and only two of his snarling teeth popped out of his mouth and onto the ground. The taller one was already reaching for his gun, but the black gloves were quicker and against the warm leather the shiny metal shattered in pieces on the ground. The cop pulled out his own fist, still swollen from the work of beating Lawrence, and swung it towards Eddie's chest, but the instant it touched the fine stitching, the empty alley echoed with a high-pitched scream, a cheated howl, and the hand erupted in a fine mesh of red. The jacket's fabric had scraped away a layer of skin. Blood ran down the policeman's hand and onto his nails, and he looked like he'd just visited one of the fussy little salons that Lola's performers loved.

The shorter cop was fumbling at the clunky hand-held radio on his belt, but Eddie's gloved hands grabbed the crackling thing and smashed it into a heap of metal at the policeman's feet. Eddie wasn't even breathing hard. The knot of fear that forever coiled inside his chest had disappeared, and in its place he could feel hot rage, from all the times he'd had to cover up parts of himself, at having to hide whenever the bulls drew near, his fury at them for fouling the sweetest moment he'd ever known. It had all tightened into a leather fist, had poured from his chest and into the woven cloth. The cloth that all week had seemed to know what Eddie wanted, what he needed, before Eddie himself ever had.

May these serve you well, Leslie had said.

The shorter cop was now scrabbling, his scraped hands reaching for the police radio in the car, and Eddie's black-gloved hands were steady as they closed over it, cutting off the crackle and static that might summon more punishing fists, and then they slipped over the shiny metal until what sang out was something altogether different.

Nobody was standing at the dirty windows to see a brown-skinned man and his gloved black hands picking up two cops, both bloodied and bruised, and standing them both upright and facing each other. Nobody saw the gloves press a set of raw knuckles around a uniformed waist and lock a dripping red palm around one scraped pink and white, an embrace that would not release, no matter how much the cops pulled and strained to escape. Nobody saw their eyes widen like a trapped animal's, or their mouths open with an angry roar that Eddie pressed into silence with the touch of his glove. Nobody saw their kicking feet begin to dance to the boogie-woogie now blaring out from the police radio: the Boswell Sisters, their sugary voices in perfect harmony singing "Cheek to Cheek," while the feet had to dance and dance, and the hands had to hold each other, and the two bloodied bodies swayed to the tune.

Only the walls and the windows saw Eddie pull a frozen Lawrence from where he had stood utterly still watching the impossible, and stumble with him past the cop car's open door. Eddie took a breath to say something, though he had no idea what, and Lawrence kissed his open mouth, a short spark, a flash.

"We were never here," Lawrence said, his lips already beginning to swell.

"And this never happened," Eddie finished, as if supplying the lyrics to a familiar song, and they headed along an empty Telegraph Avenue to catch the streetcar—the streetcar that would shut down at the end of the year, the bright metal sawed into pieces and turned into scrap. They passed the closed bookshop and next to it a window display covered in dust. The arched door was shut but ready to swing open again, the lights ready to wink on, whenever they were needed.

Eddie pulled off the black gloves so he could feel the heat of Lawrence's hand against his own, and the two of them moved along under the glowing streetlights. They left behind them two terrified dancers, their feet waltzing and tangoing and swinging all night, in a puddle of the blood they'd shed.

Author's note: there was no bar in Oakland in the late 1940s called Lola's; the only two gay bars that I could identify that operated in that time period were the White Horse in Berkeley and the Hilltop Bar in East Oakland, which opened sometime in the 1950s. Lola's is an invention for the purpose of this story, very loosely based on the real Mona's in San Francisco's North Beach, which opened in 1936.

The Nightmare Box

June 19, 1970
Friday

John arrives at exactly 3:47, carrying the nightmare box.

He's nine minutes late, but my blood has been screaming for cigarettes since Mrs. Ortíz, my 3:00, all choking perfume and sharp elbows, haunting herself with the ghost of her son. She always spends the first few minutes telling me how I'm a crook and a charlatan and a con artist, and only then can she settle into my pink armchair to talk about the little messages she's sure came from him. The crack in the face of her kitchen clock is his sorrow that he didn't have time to give her grandchildren; the purple hyacinths at the garden store are his forgiveness for the list of motherly failings she seems to have memorized. She always works herself up to angry again before her half hour is done, tossing her crumpled $9 onto the table like used tissues and slamming my front door when she goes. As if her anger could change a thing, could make her son any less dead. You shouldn't be made of such glass, I want to tell her. It just cuts everyone when you shatter. Make yourself out of stone instead;

it's a cliché for a reason. And then I smooth out the creases of the bills.

I've looked in my empty pack of Newports probably twenty times already when I hear the creak of the stairs. The wood on the bottom step has been cracking for weeks and the landlord is in no hurry to fix it. I wonder if he knew who John was, would it get fixed any faster, but that's not how this works.

The nightmare box is first through the door, gripped by pink hands shoving aside my beaded curtains, followed by a bland white man in a narrow suit and slim black tie.

"Serena? I'm Daniel. Good to see you." He doesn't acknowledge my raised eyebrows.

"Weren't you John last time?"

"Certainly not."

He's looking right at me as he settles into the chair, daring me to challenge him, as if the second he left last time I didn't grab a sheet of note paper and write down the name I heard. Before I lit my lighter to it and watched the smoke curl into the air.

Whenever John/Daniel—before that I'm almost positive it was James—parts the beaded curtains, it's like he undergoes some sort of transformation, wiping away anything that might make him stick out in my memory, and he becomes bland as margarine, smooth as wax. His second visit I spotted a Band-Aid on his right ankle when he crossed his legs, and for a heartbeat his face slipped out of its calm, like a wave passing through still water. Today must be quite the challenge for him: Wax figures sweat in the heat, and my electric fan broke yesterday. I smell the sweat before I see it, patches spreading on the black suit, blue sheen from one too many passes with an iron on high.

I gave him the nightmare box seven months ago, telling him I'd blessed it specially and he should only ever use it to bring me the items I needed, when really it was just the first box I could find in the hall closet. But you can't tell people things like that; they come to me because I tell them stories, a half hour at a time, and if they wanted ordinary, they'd keep their nine dollars. When he took it from me I could see it on his face, that slight revulsion at the superstition of These People, and underneath a layer of the envy that he would deny he's ever felt in his life, an envy I could almost smell.

If he knew I was reading him, he'd probably decide it's just more of my voodoo. I can see it in his nervous walk from wherever he parked his car, the only white man for blocks around. This place in his mind must be the land of sorcery and thumping drums, where the starched rules of his Sunday school don't apply. It would never occur to him that you can read anybody if you just pay attention.

It's the fourth time in seven months that he's brought me a box and two envelopes, things he won't touch after setting them down. The envelopes are always the same white weave, the same size, the lighter one always on top. I open it now to find, again, a typed list on a single yellow sheet, a carbon copy. I imagine some secretary in a long corridor, pulling off the white and the pink copies and slipping them into folders before settling this one into the envelopes she keeps in a drawer, and then covering up her typewriter, mind on dinner with friends or stopping at the cleaner's before they close. Never a thought for the words she's committing to paper, the lists with these headings: "Deepest Fear," "Biggest Regret(s)," "Phobias," "Most Painful Loss," "Close Friends and Family Members," "Greatest Joy."

The list wraps itself around a grainy photo, a slip of paper clipped to the back, a name and an address near San Antonio Park. The man is brown-skinned and short and smiling and it looks like three or four different parts of the world came together to make his face. His face is turned towards the sun, and you can tell it's a bright day, and hot, from the beads of sweat on his arms, but he's staring straight into the light, not squinting or covering his eyes, just ready to bear it. I shiver. Then I pull the lid off the box.

It's empty. No torn edges of a child's drawing, no gloves frayed at the fingertips, no pill bottle with the label peeling off. Nothing. I stare at John Daniel whatever his name is, and his face is waxy and blank.

"Open the other one."

I feel its weight the second I pick it up. The bills are neat and crisp, as if someone went straight to the bank just before coming here and asked the teller to count them out by machine. They nestle flat against each other, and if I could, I would put my nose to them and smell something I only get when he brings them: money that's new and clean, from soft powdered hands that never have to change their own oil or scrub their own floors.

"There's $3500 in here, John."

"It's D—" he stops himself and he holds his breath and his body oh so still; I can almost hear him counting "one Mississippi, two Mississippi" inside his head before he speaks again.

"This will be more challenging than what you're used to; I think you'll see that reflected in the amount."

"That's funny, because I'd call it impossible." And I hold up the empty box, but as his eyes stay fixed on me I can feel it weigh heavier and heavier until I collapse into my chair.

"You don't mean for *me* to collect them."

"I'm afraid that will be necessary. The usual person had some … difficulties." There's not a single emotion behind that smooth face. I wonder if this is how he would talk about me if I ran into any "difficulties."

He reaches into his suit pocket and pulls out a set of keys and a square metal button, the kind that clips at your waist, with "Markham Cleaning" in ugly lettering across the top. "On Monday, you'll be cleaning the common areas at this apartment building. Or that's what you'll say if anyone asks." I am employee #132, Rosario E. Hernández, says the button. There's a fist tightening itself inside my chest. I pry the fingers open, one by one, before I let myself answer him.

"This was never what I agreed to."

"Agreements change."

Now what's in my chest feels like a fluttering bird, flapping and knocking itself around, desperate to escape. I imagine tightening the fist around its throat, its little squeaks something I know I'm supposed to listen to before they die off.

"I won't do it. And I've already told you, this doesn't work if the person who gathers the objects isn't working from their own free will."

"I think if you remember our first meeting, and what brought you to … my attention in the first place, you might find some free will." The bird's squeaks sputter and die. I wonder if he knows I was lying about the objects anyway.

"What if I get caught?"

"Then they'll call Markham Cleaning and report an employee who doesn't exist."

"I don't mean that. I mean what if somebody calls your friends, the cops."

It's a wild stab, based on not much more than his skinny little tie and the way he never settles into my chair. If he was a cop he'd take up every inch and leave me cigarette ash to clean up. Wild, but it's landed all the same. Two Mississippis. The slim hand dips into his wallet, bills nestled tight against each other, and in between them something pale and yellowed, that sends a whole surfer's delight of waves across his face. He finds a little white card and sets it next to my tarot deck.

"These people aren't known for calling the police. But if they surprise me, here you go."

I pick up the lighter envelope again, where underneath the address there's another line: *Start date 21 Jun 1970; hard deadline 25 Jun 1970*

That bird seems to have revived itself, because now it's squeaking through my throat.

"I have four nights?"

"Three, actually." He glances down at the bills, as if to ask how I could still be complaining. "This is the apartment of the friends hosting him. He arrives this weekend. And he needs to be completely out of commission by the 25th. Next Thursday. I'd say no later than 5 p.m."

I stand up, looking for a window I can throw open, but they're all shoved up as far as they go. I toss the squawking bird out of my chest entirely, imagine instead a desk where I stack up the bills on one side and the hours on the other, as they stubbornly refuse to add up.

"I can't work that fast."

"Except when you can. Mario Campbell."

It's a memory I've refused to touch for more than two months. Part-time deacon at his church, robes neatly ironed, the faint smell of peppermint soap, his calloused hand shaking mine after the service. The last one he would ever attend in his life, thanks to that single touch. I stare at the tarot cards, nothing left I can say.

John stands up now; he's done with me. He scribbles a few lines on a note pad he pulls from his pocket and dismisses me with a nod, like we've just finished arranging for someone to repair his television. The bead curtains sway as he goes.

I hear Mr. Davies, my 4:00, tapping that cane he really doesn't need but that sometimes grants him pity. I guess he'll settle for that instead of respect. I toss everything into the nightmare box and slip it underneath the table just as the cane makes it to the top of the steps. I really need a cigarette.

Monday
9:35 a.m.

The morning sun is bright and almost taunting me as I walk up towards the address John gave me, a hulking complex on East 19th, and I've never felt as empty and hollow as I do right now. If anyone saw me they'd wonder why Markham was hiring junkies as cleaning ladies: I haven't slept since Thursday night and I've bitten my nails so bad my hands look like red claws.

In my closet I keep a box with every dollar that I got from John Daniel James or whoever he is, untouched and folded inside a can of Bustelo. Next to the can is a stack of little yellowed clippings I should have burned a long time ago, horrid symbolism or not. The story they tell is what led John to my door, what spun me away from home the day I turned eighteen. It's what keeps me from tossing the can into a duffel bag with a case of Newports and a new city plucked from my mind like roulette. I could go to New Orleans, New Mexico, New York, and he'll find me. As I pull open the heavy front door, that can and those clippings are rattling against each other, one screaming at me to run and the other just laughing and laughing at my dumb ass.

It's easy to let myself into the super's office, dark and abandoned on a Monday morning, just as my instructions said. The fist in my heart is back, pounding and pounding as if against a locked door as I grab the cleaning cart and steal an empty banker's box, my nightmare box for today. For just a moment the fist slackens as I fumble over the file cabinet and find no skeleton key: *Sorry, John or whatever you're calling yourself today; I guess the nightmares will have to wait.* And then the light through the blinds catches the key, hidden on the side, winking at me.

Nobody sees me let myself into Apartment 12, a corner unit, every window thrown open to the heat but still smelling like incense and dirty dishes and something else faint on the air, like the herbs my Tíabuela Carmen used to burn, herbs with names I've managed to forget. There's a bulletin board stuffed with paper menus and pictures, and I see the same young couple in most of them. Leather jackets and goofy hairdos, picket signs behind them in nearly every one. This must be their apartment, and their friend is my mark, the one whose black duffel bag is spread across the couch, white T-shirts and books spilling out. This place reminds me of those kids waving leaflets on Telegraph. Books all over the table, the sofa, the floor: *Guerilla Warfare*, *The Prison Notebooks*, *The Wretched of the Earth*, the pages all dog-eared and the covers creased. And flyers: "Support the National Liberation Front of Vietnam!" "Pa'lante: the 13-Point Program of the Young Lords Party," "A People's Tribunal: What Really Happened to Chairman Fred Hampton?" I know I need to grab what I came for and get out, but I can't help flipping through. They can't be more than a few years younger than me, but they're like children, with their dreams of changing the world. They haven't lived very long in this one if they think a few marches are going to change a thing. Maybe they should ask Martin Luther King how that went.

I leave behind a copy of the *Little Red Book*—what, do they give these out in some kind of starter kit?—but I grab a black sock from the duffel bag and a button that proclaims "Real Men Support Women's Rights!" His greatest joy is music, the carbon list told me, and, sure enough, there's a little cardboard box of guitar strings. I slide one out and toss it into the box, and it clangs against the button clasp.

And then I see it. On the fridge, wrinkled and stained: a funeral program with a date from two months back. Mario Campbell, the man with calloused hands and peppermint soap. I shook his hand on a Sunday and by that Wednesday he was dead in the streets, after tearing his hair and screaming about dead Vietnamese kids who would never forgive him. Here he is at a Black Panther free breakfast program, at the head of a row of smiling children. Maybe he'd hoped if he gave out enough cornbread and milk he could fill the hole he made in the world, the children who met the end of his gun. On the back page of the funeral program is a photo of him with the man whose apartment I'm standing in, the man who burns incense and doesn't wash his dishes. I've never met this man, but I've already taken one of his friends away forever, and in the box on the carpet is everything I need to take away one more.

This is the worst time I can think of for the past to try and tug at me with its cold hands. But here I am, remembering that before Mario Campbell there was Anthony Walker. Anthony learned that you lose your mind when you never let yourself sleep. He's at Napa State Hospital on an involuntary hold that nobody's going to lift any time soon. If I could, I'd tell him to never piss the nurses off bad enough to end up in the hydrotherapy rooms. But I don't think he'd want to hear it from the one who sent him there.

Before Anthony Walker there was Stephon Clark. Nearly four years sober and after weeks of my nightmares he shot those years up right inside his arm. Now he's like Alice in Ghettoland, looking at the world from the inside of a hypodermic needle, bobbing along, seeing Dodos in the gutter bums and Jabberwocks in the alley cats.

There's a white card in my pocket, with a white man's phone number, and an orange phone on the wall. What if I picked it up right now, spun the dial? Would a secretary answer, maybe the one who types up those lists? What does she tell herself about what they're for? (And what do *you* tell yourself? The bird squawks in my chest.) What would I say to John if he came to the phone? "Hey, man, funny coincidence. Turns out Mario Campbell hung around the Panthers, and looks like this next guy does too. What about Stephon Clark and Anthony Walker? Anything you want to tell me, whatever your name is?"

Like it was listening, the orange phone rings, vibrating against the wall. I slam the door behind me and get the fuck out of there.

I've almost made it out of the building, the lid on the nightmare box sealed tight, the Markham Cleaning badge scratching at my waist, and inside me that Bustelo can, clanging at me to run. And then, on the other side of the front door, there's my mark. Héctor Miranda. The man folded in my pocket, who wasn't supposed to be back here before noon.

"Hey, sister, let me help you with that door. They're not working you too hard, are they?"

I shake my head and stare at my feet, but playing the terrified Latin maid doesn't work when the other person's Latin too. When I'm through the door he smiles and reaches for the bag at his hip and hands me a flier, still warm from the mimeograph machine. "If you're not working later this week, try and see about this event? We're all stronger when we stand up together. Bring your kids if you've got 'em. We have child care." He strides on down the hall, humming a song I know right away. It's Santana, "Soul Sacrifice," a song that always sounds like freedom to me. The way he's walking looks like freedom. Like he belongs here. Like he belongs anywhere. Like he could walk into any room and everybody would shut up and listen. I see why they're so afraid of him, especially when I read the flier in my hand.

"Brothers and Sisters, All Nationalities Together in the Struggle Against Imperialism! A historic event for multiracial revolutionary unity!" I've never heard of the Young Lords, the Young Patriots, Yellow Peril, the Gay Liberation Front, or the Movimiento Estudiantil de Chicanos de Aztlán, but they're all hosting, every group bringing a speaker. Together with the

Black Panthers. The speaker for the Young Lords came from New York for this event, the flier says. And I've been assigned to make sure the last time he'll ever sleep peacefully in his life was last night, to take him out of commission before he gets on the stage, in three days' time. Thursday, June 25th, 6:00 p.m.

Monday
10:29 p.m.

The Jubilee is on a block by itself, two little streets and an alley cutting it off from every other building nearby, and I can't help it but it makes me think of a vulnerable child surrounded by bullies. There's no sign. The door's a regular apartment door, with a peephole that blinks dark when I knock. There's no response, not even a "what do you want?" When I shout Theresa's name I can hear the clink of a chain loosening, and the door opens to a room almost as dark as outside. "I'll tell Theresa you're here," the woman tosses over her shoulder, and I take the only open seat at the bar, next to two women who drop each other's hands instantly when I sit down.

The bartender and I size each other up, but she's better at this than I am. She's in the wrong line of work, I want to tell her. Unlike me she doesn't have to pretend she's not doing it. In fact she makes sure I see her doing it, and whatever test this is, I've barely gotten a C.

"It's okay, Betty; she's cool," a voice reassures her from over my shoulder. I haven't heard my cousin's voice in eight years, if you don't count one or two awkward conversations on the phone. I'm not sure if she'll hug me or throw her beer in my face. I'm not sure which I want. She doesn't do either; she just motions to a set of stairs in the back and leads me up to a narrow hallway on the second floor, where she opens a door to a dingy apartment, a battered fridge holding not much more than beer and jars of olives. I remember how she used to steal them from salads when we were kids.

I have no idea how to catch up on those years, how to close the distance from passing the pasteles at dinner to passing an ashtray back and forth at her rusty kitchen table, the faint sound of someone losing at pool in the bar below. Every question I ask gets one word for an answer, two if I'm lucky, and when I finally let them drop I'm not sure which one of us is more relieved. She lights herself one of my Newports and waits for me to begin.

I can't tell her the whole story, and my brain keeps tripping over the things I can't say. Even then it takes us three beers, and she keeps interrupting to pull at what I'm leaving out.

"Shit," Theresa sighs out with the smoke. "So that's why Tíabuela Carmen spent so much time with you. She knew you could do it too."

"Yeah. That's why they stopped letting her visit."

"And can't you just tell that man you won't do his bidding? Not this time?"

"I told you. He could find me."

"How'd he find you in the first place?"

"The fire. The police report."

"Jesus, prima." She stabs out her cigarette and immediately lights another. "You mean when you killed that man?"

That man. The manager of the restaurant where my father worked. I'd never meant for him to burn. I'd only wanted him to feel what my father felt, that relentless cold when a walk-in freezer locked him in, six hours until someone rescued him, because the manager wouldn't bother to fix the tricky latch. I couldn't know that my victim would run howling into the restaurant and light everything desperately on fire, anything to warm himself from the cold that wasn't really there. I couldn't know that next to the walk-in freezer were barrels and barrels of cheap alcohol that the manager was selling for a quick buck, that went up in flames like a dry Christmas tree.

"That was when they sent you away, wasn't it."

I can't answer her. If I even breathe too deep, it'll all come pouring out. A gibbering seventeen-year-old girl, screaming that it was all her fault, she'd been too angry and made the nightmare too strong. The iced sheets, layer on layer, strapping me in for hours until the nurses thought I was ready to behave. The woman I saw wrapped in white canvas, thudding at the padded walls; I thought they'd removed her arms, which in a way they had, because she couldn't get them back until she'd been good. My mother and father on visiting days, letting me beg and plead and cry to never do it again, ever, if they would just let me come home. They finally took me back after three months, but we all knew they could change their minds any time.

But I've never told Theresa any of this, and I can't start now. She lights another cigarette and blows smoke into the violet sky.

"So how much is he paying you?" The faucet's dripping behind her, the cracked linoleum thick with dirt. I can't tell her I could rent this apartment for a year with what I make from one nightmare.

"Must be a lot then. And you can do this to anyone? Any time?"

It takes me a second to understand that note in her voice.

"You don't need to be afraid of me. I'd never—"

"Oh, so you do have a line you won't cross."

I wish I could storm out, but she's sitting between me and the door.

"Theresa. You're my *family*."

"What's that word supposed to mean to me? You remember who you're talking to, right?"

This hurts, but I deserve it. We were both seventeen when her parents kicked her out, letting her follow her girlfriend to Oakland and then call them sobbing, begging for money when the girlfriend kicked her out too, and I never spoke up for her, never called. I couldn't. Any time I thought of it, I remembered those iced sheets.

"I have my own life now, Theresa. If you came in the middle of the night asking for a floor to crash on or a meal to eat, I'd give it to you, no questions asked. When did those goofy motherfuckers ever put food on my table?"

"First of all, prima, those goofy motherfuckers do put food on tables. For children. And second of all, they want to make a world where everybody does."

I drag Newport smoke into my lungs. "You don't really believe that."

"Not really. I think in a few months they're going to cut off their funny hairdos and stop marching and get a real job. But why do you suddenly care about them anyway? Why now?"

I don't cry anymore. There's no point. But Theresa doesn't know that, and when the drop slides down my face she probably thinks it's a good thing. Like for a second I was a normal person.

"I didn't know. I didn't know."

"Huh. And now that you do?"

I shouldn't have come here. I stand up to go and she tugs at my shirt and pulls me back. She's worn and tired and looks ten years older than me, but I'd switch places with her in a second if I could. She calls me the name I've left behind for eight years, and maybe that's really the only reason I came.

"Ana María. Don't act like you don't choose where you draw the line."

⸎

Wednesday
6:33 p.m.

Mrs. Saunders has just left, glowing and happy because I told her that her dead husband loved her hideous dress, when I hear the building door slam and someone taking the stairs two at a time. John tosses the beaded curtains aside so hard they knock a tiny clay orisha onto the floor.

"Héctor Miranda is bright-eyed and cheerful and is meeting right now with a gang of degenerates from around the country. And don't tell me you've lost your touch, because for months you've been the most reliable one we've got." I should get you angry more often, John. You don't look any more human, but you start spilling things you know damn well you shouldn't.

"Well? Do you care to explain?"

I stand now and face him, the yellow table the only thing between us. "Care to explain why you never told me what all those men have in common?"

The expression on his face looks like he put his hand on a doorknob and it started to talk.

"What? What do you care? Are you suddenly above all this now? Because I've given you thousands of dollars that say otherwise." He's right. It's not like I'm Theresa, tired and proud of her worn linoleum and her empty fridge. Choosing just where she draws the line.

I stand very still and lock my eyes on his until he takes a deep breath, taking in the candles still burning, the orisha he cracked. I can see him realizing he'll have to reason with me, and he has no idea how.

"Look. Serena. You're a smart girl. Don't let these people fool you. They talk all these great fairy-tale ideas, but the reality is, they're bloody and violent. They killed police officers. They have connections with North Korea and Red China. They bring drugs into your ghettos; did you know that?"

"You think I care what someone shoots up their arm?"

"Jesus. Then maybe think about what else is at stake. Can you make yourself care about that? These people are the most dangerous group in the country, and you have the power to stop them. No trail for the press to follow, no messy scenes that the agitators keep trying to dig up. The wounds can heal. We can come together again as a nation. For Christ's sake, we made you people into Americans. Why is it so hard for you to act like one now?"

Oh, did you now, John? That was the wrong thing to say to me. I can count Mississippis too. My dad's aunt Tillie was living there when the Klan shot up her house. And when they marched in their little parades it was the American flag they were waving. The same flag the soldiers waved when they came to Puerto Rico, shooting up my grandmother's island, taking it for theirs. The same flag you want me to defend.

I still say nothing, letting him twist. Instead I bend down to pick up the orisha, the jagged line running right through its center. The slightest pressure and it'll crack in two.

"What, you want more money? Is that it?" I don't answer, because I don't know. Is there a number that could choke off the sound of voices rising in prayer on that Sunday, the part-time deacon shaking my hand, the smell of peppermint soap? Was there an amount of free breakfast that could have banished the dying screams from Mario Campbell's nightmares? Maybe, until I made sure they followed him into the daylight. Is there an amount that could banish that helpful smile, that "they're not working you too hard, are they, sister?" I'm afraid there might be, and if he lays just the right amount on the table I'll know what it is.

I do know this, though: The last time he opened up his wallet something in there nearly fell out, something that he really shouldn't keep in there any more but he can't bear not to. Something that really could crack everything open, if I could make it fall into my hands.

So when he lays out the envelope on the table—he was prepared for this—I open it, count the money, glance at his wallet. He wants to say no, but I don't move, don't take my eyes off of the leather, so he has to open it back up, and in a rush of exasperation he pulls out every bill and thrusts them into my hand. And when he does the yellowed thing falls out too, floating its way to the floor, while his disgusted eyes lock on me. Every second of the last eight years, all my hiding every emotion where even I can't find them, they all come together to help me in the next few heartbeats, to keep my face from reacting and my eye muscles from following its journey onto the floor. I pick up the money instead, and my heart really is thudding when I count it all up. He shoves the wallet into his pocket, emptied now. I don't pray, but if I did it would be that whatever he's included, it isn't enough. I'm pretty sure he's praying right now that it is.

I don't give him an answer; instead I just nod, that same dismissive jerk of the head he used on me before, a transaction, pure and simple. Everyone has their price.

Once he's crossed the rotten step, I pick up what fell. It's a picture, so creased it's threatening to split. A little baby in a ruffly dress, with the Alameda ferry just behind her, and at her feet someone's written, in school teacher handwriting: "Ariel, three months old, April 1969." The man holding her is John, on his face a wide smile that I've never seen, and a wedding ring bright and shiny on his hand, on the same finger that now has a faint little crease.

Maybe little Ariel is somewhere toddling and happy, holding the hand of the woman who wrote that flowery script. But I don't think so. It's in John's face, the bright sunny beaming at whoever was taking that picture, and the emptiness that never leaves it now, and the waves that threatened to break when his hands grazed the yellowed edges. I think the little girl in the picture is long gone. I think she's nothing more than a ghost.

Thursday
10:09 a.m.

The microfilm machine at the library acts like it hates me. The reels keep slipping out of the stupid feeder in the back, and when I drop one onto the floor I curse louder than I'm supposed to in here, summoning the librarian in her little clicky heels.

"May I help you?" Does anybody say that and actually mean it? But she slides the reels into the machine, smooth as her coral lipstick, and she turns the knobs until the Alameda Times-Star is sliding past us, day after day, backwards in time. When I ask her to please slow down she looks like she wishes libraries had those signs about refusing service to anyone.

"What are you looking for, dear?"

"Um, just interesting things." We both want her to go away, but she just sighs and moves the knob slower. My watch says I've been at this for half an hour, and I have no idea how much time I have left, and then I see what I came for, on the next-to-last page, gone almost before I can catch it.

It's a birth announcement, January 4, 1969: Ariel Renee Carter, born to Ellen May Carter and Christian Joseph Carter of Alameda, California. And not five months after that, she's there again, same tiny text, neat black and white, but the story leading back to the beginning, where my grandma told me we all crawl back someday.

Ariel died peacefully in her sleep, no explanation found. One doctor had a tentative diagnosis, what they were beginning to call Sudden Infant Death Syndrome. I nearly laugh out loud when I read this, doctors needing to label what everyone already knows. Your baby died and nobody knows why. Here, have a name. Everything needs its neat little box. Including me, because now I know enough about John—Christian—to fill out every one of those columns myself, no typewriter needed.

Greatest joy, closest family, most painful loss. And an object, just one this time, but somehow I think it will be enough.

———

The drugstore has compact mirrors that sit open on their sides, mirrors looking into each other's faces, like a funhouse, in sizes that stack up each bigger than the next, and I buy every one. They sit heavy in my bag as I ride the bus to Sears and ask the counter girl for a slim black tie, and she wrinkles up her nose: "Like those FBI guys?" Yes, sister. Like that.

I find the dollhouse in their toy department. When the girl asks if I need furniture I stop for a minute and set down the weight of the bags and let my hands caress the velvet-backed chairs, the tiny plates in the sideboard, as if I'm about to set the table for eight. My parents are coming, my grandma, Theresa and her parents and her brother Jimmy, who never drove his car into a ditch. And none of them turned their backs on Theresa for kissing a girl under the steps of her father's house. I've always lived at home, and nobody ever signed a judge's order to wrap my arms around myself and thud me into a padded wall. We're all here and the lechón is ready, the crickets singing outside.

"Miss?"

I put the chairs back where they belong.

"Just the house, thank you."

"Do you need it gift-wrapped?"

No, but I let her do it anyway. I count out three of John's twenties and slip her $5 when she hands back my change. The sunshine glints off the ribbons and a few women smile at me on the bus home.

Tonight Héctor Miranda will take the stage and talk of revolutionary unity and changing the world and the kinds of things children talk about before they know any better, the things they can believe are real if they just weave those dreams tight enough around themselves. Like Mrs. Ortíz needs to believe that a cracked kitchen clock is really her son. But Héctor will be standing, and walking, and whole, and whatever he dreams about tonight, I will have nothing to do with it. Will John be watching from the crowd? When will he know that yes, there is a line, and he and I are both on the same side of it, staring each other down? He wants to believe he's firmly in the camp of the good. I know neither of us gets to even visit there.

I toss the Bustelo can and a change of clothes into the Sears bag and tack up a "Closed" sign on the door downstairs. And on the front room table I lay out everything I'll need. I caress the creased picture, the little girl's smiling face. She has a dimple in each cheek, and I imagine her father watching her sleep, waiting for her to wake up so he can see them brighten her face again. The way they never will.

I put her at the end of the dollhouse's long hallway and then lay the mirrors facing each other along every wall, so he'll see her face reflected again and again. Then I slip the black tie out of its tissue paper and tie it around her throat. Now everywhere he turns he will imagine himself yanking it around her neck, choking her life away. From his dreams for the future, his future, choking the life out of his own hope. The way he used me to snuff out those little gasps of hope for the future. Doesn't matter how ridiculous those folks look to me, their enormous hairdos and identical little jackets, their fairy tale about changing the world. They're still braver than I'll ever be. And they will never belong to John, or Daniel, or James, or Christian Carter of Alameda, California.

I imagine him tonight, drifting off to sleep in some narrow little bed, crumbs of TV dinner still clinging to his chin, and as the nightmare comes on him sweet and strong, as he stares at his own face reflected everywhere, watching his own hands around her throat, he knows it's a nightmare, and it changes nothing; he can't wake up. And when he runs screaming from the dollhouse, covering his eyes, begging for escape, he'll see nothing but the rows of candles I lit all around, the cracked orisha at the center of a wall of flame. Like what Great-Aunt Tillie saw when the Klan shot up her house. Like what Fred Hampton saw, the gunfire erupting through every window.

It's never occurred to him that we might turn our powers onto him, has it? Imagine that kind of blindness. As soon as he doesn't need us, we disappear.

He doesn't know yet that if he ever drifts off in meetings or lets his eyes flicker to the rhythm of a projector in the dark, he'll see her face and his hands, and he'll be helpless to pull them off. Something else, that he's never been curious enough to know, is that when I tie him and his daughter together, she will follow him into the daylight. Asleep or awake, he'll never be able to leave her behind, or his hands around her neck, this image that he knows isn't real but won't be reasoned away. That's where I live, Christian. People leave behind reason when they come through the beaded curtains. They come for the stories. And I'm writing you the best one.

The anger is thudding at my chest and it feels wonderful. No fluttering this time, just black wings finding their way to the sun. Downstairs I hear the sigh of the front door and someone on the bottom step, and who knows if it's the police, tipped off to an easy warrant for bad checks, or a trio of nurses with their straitjacket handy. Maybe Christian himself, but that would be just fine. All he has to do is let me touch him just once. Or maybe it's my Thursday at 4, Miss DeAngelis, a whirlwind who may or may not read the sign telling her to come back tomorrow. I hear the crack from below as the step finally gives in.

Will They Disappear

I'm only fourteen and I don't look like much and I've lived in more foster homes than I can count on two hands but I've learned a lot of lessons anyway. Like: playing dumb is a real smart strategy, most of the time. So is playing weak, only showing my strengths when it's the right time. I didn't do too good a job with that one, but if the names "Jessica and Elizabeth Love" ring a bell, then I think you might just forgive me.

I was different from the other kids in every foster home for a couple of reasons, but here's the biggest one: I can make things disappear. No living things, even though I admit it, I did try. Just on a potato bug. I was kind of relieved it didn't work, honestly. I can't do it with anything big, like whole buildings, probably because there might be living things in them. It's only little stuff, like making a homework assignment disappear so I could say I never got it, and one foster father's keys I kept taking away because I knew he was cheating and ... okay, maybe I did mean that one to hurt? The family thought I was stealing, and that's how I got kicked out.

I can't make them reappear. I also don't know where they go. I didn't used to care, but now that I'm older I keep imagining it. Are they all sitting in some back room somewhere, gathering dust? Are they dust? Also, when I wish something away, something else appears. I don't know if they're all coming out of the same funny place. I've never pictured a dark tunnel, a damp cave, the kind of places inhabited by trolls with hairy feet and green teeth. Instead I picture a store room somewhere, neat rows of shelves, the stock doors rolling up and down whenever new things appear. I think it's because that's what I really want. Everything in order, everything clean and bright. A long table with room for everyone I got attached to in all the homes I've been in. Everybody doing their chore—chop the lettuce, wash the dishes—and eating three meals every day. Someone to tuck us in and call us back if we left our dirty plate on the table. It's what I thought I was getting when the Loves took me in.

***

I wonder if I spent a lot of time in an actual stock room when I was little. I have no idea: The records of my life begin when I was two. If you can believe the Stanislaus County Department of Social Services, they swung open the door of their office at exactly 9:01 in the morning and spotted two-year-old me, standing in the cold in a pink sweatsuit and sparkly shoes. Waiting patiently, happy to enjoy hot chocolate when they brought me inside. Newspaper articles, TV spots, my plump brown cheeks and pigtails smiling for the cameras, turned up nothing: no tearful mother regretting her choice to drop me off in the lot, no grateful family with throats hoarse from looking all night. Nobody could figure out how a child as well-cared for as me could just fall out of a family and not be missed. My clothes were clean and smelled of laundry soap; my skin was healthy, my hair shiny. When the social workers asked me to play a game of pattycake I indulged them, like that was a game I didn't care for, thank you very much, but I would humor them just this once. I could suck up chocolate milk and hot chocolate like a fish, though, and they couldn't figure out how I'd managed to eat three whole packages of Otis Spunkmeyer cookies in less than five minutes. They found me covered in crumbs, a look on my face like, "I was wondering when you'd show up."

After weeks they realized they needed a birth certificate for me, because apparently you don't exist without one, and no bureaucracy—there's a word I learned early—can tolerate an un-birth-certificated child. One of the social workers, who apparently loved Greek myths, decided to name me Athena. She sprung full-grown from her father's head one afternoon, which was as good an explanation as any for how I got there. After they talked to lawyers and experts and took way too many x-rays they decided I was somewhere between 24 and 26 months. They could write "unknown" for father and mother, but I still needed a birth date, so they stuck the year precisely two years before. The date was the same day I appeared at the edge of the parking lot, like I didn't really exist in the world until someone official was there to see it.

Applications were flooding in to take in Baby Girl Moses, including of course lots of evangelical families, and I have to think that my brown skin was like an added bonus. Extra Jesus points for saving me not from the bulrushes but the acacia tree outside the front door.

I stayed with my first family for five years, until I was seven. I remember it mostly in colors, in feelings. Cookie dough spoons scraping the sides of a bowl, toast for breakfast every morning, tomato soup I couldn't stand, scratchy grass in the backyard, the neighbor's dog I snuck pieces of cheese to, pink tongue licking my hand through the bars. Wednesday night church service, already half asleep when we got home, my arms dangling over my foster father's shoulders as he carried me inside and tucked me into bed. As far as I know, nothing ever disappeared there.

I don't remember anyone explaining to me that I had to move on. I don't remember anyone sitting me down and telling me that they'd got pregnant, a miracle they'd thought they'd never see. I don't remember asking why I couldn't just stay. I have to think that some conversation happened. That they didn't just do what some adults actually thought helped: lying and telling me they were going to the store, and then never coming back. Oh, we'll shield her from the panic. I have to think that they didn't just quietly pack up my things and wave goodbye, tears in their eyes, sadness soothed by the swelling of her belly and the kicking of their new child through the skin. If the conversation did happen, did I just block it out?

It's one thing to get a foster placement when you're two and adorable and the story of Athena in the bulrushes is national news. It's another when you're seven and you've started wetting the bed for the first time, and you keep sneaking out the front door of wherever they send you, trying to find your way back to your home. I think it was three or four places I bounced back and forth from in two years, a damp little brown ball.

I remember the first thing I made disappear. It was harmless: All I had left on my plate was eggplant, eggplant I had to finish if I was going to get brownies for dessert. I stared at it and I wished it would just go away, and then I fell onto the floor and it was gone. I've since learned how to not fall. It makes me light-headed, like that feeling you get when you stand up after you've been sitting still too long. But I'd made a mistake, because the whole plate was gone too, and I couldn't explain why. I didn't get any brownies. And I also couldn't explain why there was a pool noodle in the washing machine, in a house that had no pool anywhere near.

I went overboard at first, once I figured it out. Wouldn't you? I made my dirty socks disappear, and later on that night with no warning a pair of ancient encyclopedias, from the 1980s at least, showed up inside the bathtub. I learned to wish away the eggplant—I don't care who says they like eggplant, they're lying—but not the plate it was on. But it was a gamble. I might make the eggplant disappear and then a little green frog would start hopping around the living room. Or I'd wish away my bratty foster brother's favorite game cartridge and a dead orchid would crash onto the floor.

Sometimes what showed up was scary. When I made my teacher's hat disappear, a spider crawled over my sandaled foot. A warning from the bright tunnel? Another time what showed up was a jar of formaldehyde, a word I knew because I read every entry in those encyclopedias (Volumes E and F.) I thought of frogs splayed out and ready for the scalpel, of the frog that hopped over the sofa. There was what looked like a floating candy heart in the jar, red and pickled and bobbing up and down.

When I was ten I began to see myself in books, sort of. I was in a home that locked us out until 6:30 when the mom got home from work, and so I spent hours every day at the library. You'd be amazed how many books you can read if you find a little corner and curl up for three hours straight, especially when the librarian starts conveniently walking by and leaving little piles like breadcrumbs. I read the one about the teenage girl who could move things with her mind and got revenge against the bullies. It was fun but it didn't matter how long I tried to make the brownies across the room come my way; they weren't interested. After I read the one about the little girl who could start fires I actually stood outside and stared at the dry grass for so long that I missed the recess bell. The other kids made fun of me for a month after that. A month is a long time when you're ten.

When I was twelve I finally landed at a group home, the bottom of a drain I'd been circling for years. This home wasn't as scary as the stories the other kids used to tell, but, even so, things started going missing every day. For the first time in my life I was openly cruel about it. The little girl who shared my room could barely see without her coke-bottle glasses, and I didn't take those, but I did wish away a ratty old T-shirt. She'd said the shirt belonged to her mother, who was going to take her back as soon as she got out of jail. I wished the shirt away and the little girl's colored pencils too, and that night in bed a catfish skeleton showed up at my feet, little bits of flesh still clinging to the bone. I was awake when it did, because I was listening to the little girl crying. I tossed the fish in the kitchen trash, risking a demerit because we weren't allowed out of our beds after lights out, and after I washed my feet (risking one more) I tapped gently on the little girl's shoulder and asked if she needed a hug. She nodded and I let her curl up against me, wetting my shirt with her tears. That morning a stuffed turtle showed up on top of the dresser and I handed it to the girl, who didn't ask any questions about where it came from. That's one of the great things about little kids: still young enough to believe in magic.

I learned something else then: It's one thing to bend so easy that I can be mute at one house or stupid at another one, especially with adults who think they're the same thing anyway. It's another thing to let myself get mean to a scared little kid. I was mad that I had to teach myself this lesson, but I figured if I started getting mad about everything that's happened to me, that would be a really long thread to pull, and I'd end up with just a mess of tangled threads in my lap, and guess who'd be cleaning it up?

It was maybe three months after the stuffed turtle, and I'd figured out that it was a mistake to let myself turn twelve without being adopted. Nobody wants an awkward older kid, no matter what famous story she has. So I couldn't believe my luck when Jessica and Elizabeth Love showed up.

They came into the visiting room, patting my hand, flashing pictures of their ranch-style home in Modesto, of the five children who lived with them there, all either adopted or on their way to it. I tried not to let myself get excited at the pictures of the family, grinning and making chocolate-chip cookies, every picture tagged #rainbowtribe and #SavedbyLove.

"You've been through so much," the blonder one of them said, slipping an arm around my neck, white teeth opening wide in a smile. Pink skin against my light brown. Their pearl-gray minivan came for me the next day, two weeks before Christmas.

It was just Jessica driving, and she put on some radio news show and barely said a word the whole time, and when we got to the house she left me to huff my bags up the driveway alone. I tiptoed through the open door, and I couldn't have explained it just then, but I knew there was something wrong here. Like, deep wrong. Soaked into the wet bones of the house wrong.

There was a "Live Laugh Love" painting sticking out of one of the half-open boxes all over the room, and a rainbow afghan on the couch. The kids were all huddled around a huge coffee table in the living room, piles of books and a few tablets open in front of them, and Elizabeth told everybody to introduce themselves. Mai Anh ("we call her Maya," the Loves assured me) was nine, the youngest, and then Dev, eleven years old, tall and skinny, who used crutches he'd decorated with Flaming Unicorn stickers. ("They're a YouTube band," he said, like I'd been born yesterday.) Isaiah and DeAndre were twins, both twelve like me, and they both waved and then turned back to their books. The oldest kid was their sister Sienna; she was fourteen but looked younger than me. Except for her eyes; those belonged to a thirty-year-old single mom. All those skin tones looked like a multicultural Crayola box, and my flesh was the missing shade in the bunch.

"Is school on Christmas break already?" I asked, already knowing the answer.

"Oh, we homeschool," Jessica told me. That same smile, teeth wet and bone white.

I shared a room with Sienna and Mai Anh, and I waited until it was dark that night, the stars trying to shine through the blinds, before I opened my mouth. "Sienna, what's the deal with them? I mean, the moms?" Sienna took so long to speak, I thought she was ignoring me.

"You'll see." I could hear Mai Anh's quiet snores. "It'll be okay for a while. And then you'll see."

I thought she was just trying to scare me. I saw what she meant, soon enough.

After morning lessons Elizabeth came out of the kitchen with boxes and bowls for the kids to make gingerbread houses. Sugar glaze for glue, M&Ms in neat little bowls on the table, plates of gum drops in pink and purple, tiny licorice sticks for the chimneys. I'd never actually made gingerbread houses before, so I thought it would be like those TV shows and commercials where kids gobbled up every other piece of candy while their moms swatted them and giggled. Here, I watched Isaiah drop a gumdrop on the table and Elizabeth's eyes shot right to it. Under that blue gaze he picked up the candy and put it right on that little roof, like that was the only place it belonged.

Elizabeth was the one who wandered around in her Black Lives Matter shirt, holding her phone up high, updating the family's Instagram page. When she called out for everyone to smile, five heads swiveled toward the camera, five sets of dead eyes lit up, five sets of teeth flashed open wide.

As soon as the last photo was done the kids all jumped up, like they'd been stuck with a pin, and started cleaning up the little bowls, vacuuming the sugar off the carpet, wiping the counters until they were shining and clean. Elizabeth walked over and took each beautiful house and tossed it straight into the trash. Dish soap drizzled over each one. "Just in case," she said, and she was actually smiling.

———

I'm not going to tell everything I learned in those first few weeks. Not everything is good to talk about. I will say that it wasn't so much what they did to us but what they took away. Didn't make your bed? Miss breakfast. Fail a test from Teacher Jessica, especially if the reason was your stomach screaming at you after missing breakfast? Skip lunch. I started searching the house for little things I could disappear: a bath bead, a paper clip, a sock under the bed. I wanted to see if anything that appeared would be edible. Nothing ever was, and the night I couldn't explain the shiny white mannequin head on my dresser, the Loves put me outside on the porch overnight with a nightlight and a sleeping bag. They lived at the end of a dead-end street, and we'd never seen any neighbors on either side. No one to notice, no one to help. I didn't disappear anything for a long time after that.

———

We moved a lot, the rainbow tribe and our rulers. Partly because Elizabeth was a traveling med tech and she could stick a pin in a map and drag us all anywhere. But that's not the only reason why. Just after New Year's a social worker came and talked to the Loves on the porch. The rest of us leaned against the door to listen: something about Mai Anh's family and a bunch of calls and letters going ignored, and some relative that had been trying to see her for two years. Mai Anh rocked back and forth, Sienna holding her tight. That night we heard the panicked voices from the Loves' bedroom at the end of the house, shouting about credit card debt and foster care payments that might disappear. "And then what would we live on?" I heard Jessica scream. It was still dark when the Loves threw a bunch of boxes into our rooms and said we had half an hour to fill them. The van rattled away before it got light, and the other kids just stared out the windows like nothing had happened. I was the only one surprised.

"I don't get my hopes up anymore," said Sienna, when we got to the new place, twenty miles south of Reno. "They just move." Sienna was counting the days until she could get out of there, and try to free at least her brothers as soon as she could. I added them up with her: one thousand, four hundred, and twenty-one days. It was impossible to imagine, like a book I read about a stairwell reaching high in the sky, disappearing into the clouds.

I think we were in Nevada for three or four months, and then Elizabeth got a job in Spokane. After Spokane it was Eugene, and by that time I'd learned from Sienna: Don't bother to un-pack.

Wherever we moved, a bunch of us would go find the library. DeAndre told the Loves that getting our library cards could be a cool ritual in a new place, and we could post the pictures, hashtagging them #librarylife. "Yeah, I love adventure stories," he told me one day while we were walking on some street in Modesto, or maybe Spokane, our backpacks so heavy they were slowing us down. "But also, when I'm at the library, they leave me in peace." DeAndre spoke like a cross between a kid and an 18th-century gentleman, like the Alexandre Dumas books he'd started to read. We would bring back comics for Dev, who read the Miles Morales Spider-Man books over and over until their spines nearly broke.

It was quiet for a while in Eugene. Jessica was teaching us how to make balloon piñatas out of paper mache, and the first few times I sat next to her and that bowl of slimy white strips I want-ed to pour the whole thing over her head. But, like the library, those afternoons were little slices of peace. When we were done we took the paper mache-covered balloons and popped them, and the scratchy things kept their shape, but they were empty, hollow inside. Elizabeth propped us up for pictures, and she posted a long gushing post to Instagram. She tagged it #rain-bowtribe and #outofnothing. And, of course, #savedbyLove.

She sat at her phone, swelling up a little more every time a like or a heart popped up. The way she always did.

Then one day Dev fell and dislocated his shoulder. Maybe he said something to the doctor, or maybe that doctor noticed something the other ones never did, because a few days later a social worker came to the door. The Loves couldn't sit close enough to hear us, but they sat where they could see her reactions, which was basically the same thing. I gave the right answers, the ones we'd memorized. We all did. I was sitting there wondering what the Loves might do to Dev, who'd sworn up and down he hadn't said a thing.

And then, I don't know why, but I disappeared Jessica's Converse from the shoe cubby by the front door, while we were all in the living room. I've never figured out what made me start up again, why I listened to that wish when I'd pushed down so many of them before. I think it was Dev's face, tight with fear, while Jessica was wearing her perfect smile. When she showed the social worker to the door the sneakers were missing but she had to act like nothing was wrong. I loved watching her expression, trying to keep that sticky sweetness she wore, her face dissolving and hardening again. I wondered if something rotten would show up again, or something beautiful. Instead it was kind of neither: an Amtrak time table from 1952, half the pages highlighted and dog-eared.

Watching her face felt so good that I disappeared their "Live Laugh Love" poster that night while we were all in our beds. I was half dreaming when their bedroom door opened, and the

Loves both ran screaming out, and there was a bat, flapping and tangled in Elizabeth's hair.

I knew I was making it worse, because they got meaner the more panicked they got. But it felt so good to rattle them, finally, after I'd held it in for so long. I disappeared their faded Obama T-shirts and Jessica's signed Kamala Harris hoodie, and they knew none of us kids could have done it. The Loves kept their bedroom locked. The other kids were beginning to suspect something, but nobody had said anything to me yet. Instead they kept opening the Loves' scars, the ones I never let heal. "Maybe you need more sleep, Moms," Mai Anh started telling them. Her voice was sweet but she'd discovered *James and the Giant Peach* that year, and when the Loves couldn't hear she'd call them Aunt Sponge and Aunt Spiker. Sienna would say, "It's okay. I lose stuff too," and there'd be a little smirk at the edge of her mouth.

We moved to Oakland a few months after I turned fourteen. It was the last move, though of course nobody knew that. The Loves must have gotten another letter, another phone call, a visit they hadn't told us about. They stayed up late one night arguing when they thought we were asleep. Elizabeth was convinced that we should go back to the house where she grew up, and Jessica was trying to talk her out of it. Like that was going to work. "Babe, please. I don't have the energy to fix it up and you're going to be working. And that isn't a good place to raise kids."

Like they give a shit, Dev mouthed to me from the hallway where we crouched, listening. We'd gotten real good at communicating without sound.

"You'll see. Oakland's gotten so much better the last few years. Plus they can't even hire social workers, never mind keeping them. We might finally have some peace."

So again we packed up the van and drove eight hours to a huge house on Dover Street. The Loves had kicked the tenants out in a hurry and their stuff was still scattered in every room. Most of it went off to the dump, but there was a pile of books we passed around like it was Christmas, and a pair of roller skates that Isaiah rode all over the driveway, even after he scraped his knee raw.

The move to Oakland turned something over in me. Maybe it was the way the libraries were different, all the books I started hauling back to the house, kids with brown skin wielding magic against their oppressors. Maybe it was the murals in the neighborhood, fists of all colors raised in the air. Maybe it was just turning fourteen. But I started disappearing things all over that house. I didn't care if they punished me, and I knew I should have been afraid of something even worse than the heart-looking thing in the jar, but I wasn't. When the dead rat showed up in the medicine cabinet I grinned and then used a pair of tongs to throw it away. At dinner I served the Loves their corn with those same tongs, and then I dropped them on the floor so I'd have an excuse to wash them before I served anyone else.

I took Jessica's keys, three times, right from the hook by the door, whenever she knew the kids couldn't have done it. Elizabeth kept calling her scatterbrained, and I could see Jessica crumbling and crumbling, wondering if she really had lost her mind. One of the things that came back was a toy gingerbread house. It looked just like the ones we made at Christmas but never got to eat. When Elizabeth asked where it came from I blinked and told her, "I've always had this." The other kids still didn't know anything, not for sure, but they knew who to root against anyway. "Oh, yeah, Athena's always had that," everyone said.

That night, once it got quiet, Sienna turned to me. "So what's the story with ... you know?"

"You'll see," I answered, hoping she could hear the smile in my voice, hoping it didn't sound like a smirk. And then I wished away one of my socks, no big deal. I was ready for whatever might show up, even though I'd never forgotten that night on the porch. (On Dover Street it was the attic, stuffed with junk that could look like anything in the dark.) Then the moonlight shone through the window on a glittering disco ball, and the two of us took turns holding it up to the light, letting it sparkle on our faces. We hid it in my laundry hamper and agreed not to tell the other kids, at least not yet. Secrets were nothing new to the rainbow tribe.

I told you I was making it worse, and I was. One night I insulted dinner and dropped my plate on the floor and looked right at them both, the expression on my face saying, "punish me." I could see them casting bewildered eye signals at each other. I never broke the rules. But Elizabeth called me onto the back porch and she looked hesitant, for a second, because I didn't look afraid. I turned away so she couldn't see the wish on my face, and I heard the belt whistle through the air but it didn't land. When I turned back, her empty hand was trembling and her face was the best thing I'd ever seen. It looked like what I'd actually made disappear were her bones, and she was crumbling to dust while I watched.

So when the Loves got meaner and meaner, taking away food for almost any excuse, I knew it was kind of my fault. And my fault that DeAndre showed up one afternoon with a bag of stuff for us: bread, peanut butter, those little oranges from Trader Joe's. He'd made friends with the neighbors at the end of the block, and he'd told them we were low on food because his mothers were sick. I mean, I guess they were, if you think about it.

DeAndre said he wasn't going to go back, because the neighbors might start asking too many questions. But he did, because it was food. And I guess somewhere in there the neighbors sniffed out that something was wrong. Or maybe Mai Anh's family found the Loves again, now that we were back in California. Maybe both. Because a social worker came knocking again, and by then the Loves were both rattled and furious and arguing all the time. Maybe that's why they panicked so bad. The social worker left her card on the door in the morning and by lunchtime we were all in the van.

Elizabeth told the kids she had a headache and we needed to sit and be quiet. But our faces were all flashing at each other that something was really wrong. It was Mai Anh who pointed to the empty spots in the van, like she was reminding us that nobody actually packed any boxes this time. But then Elizabeth pulled up at a Taco Bell and for the first time ever we could order whatever we wanted. It felt so good just to eat. Plus, all of us kids were so tired. Every time the Loves shouted at each other at night it kept us awake.

The Taco Bell was the one next to the beach, in Pacifica, and afterwards we all ran around on the sand. We were already in the van when Elizabeth went back inside, and came out again with a tray of something called Berry Freezes. Mine was bright blue, and it tasted way too sweet, but as I kept drinking I didn't mind so much. I finished almost the whole thing, kind of weird when it didn't have any chocolate.

The ocean stretched off to our right as they drove south. It was the most beautiful thing I'd ever seen. The sun was shining over the waves and the van smelled of beach sand and salt. I actually fell asleep, and I came sort of awake when the van pulled into a parking lot, my mouth sticky with sugar and my thoughts swirly and far away, like the fog. The Loves were sitting there totally quiet, and my skin started almost itching, I was so sure something was off.

I kept my eyes shut, pretended I was still sleeping, and I heard the doors open and gravel crunching under their feet. Then I heard tinkling bells, the kind that stores use to announce a customer, and then I made myself count to twenty before I opened my eyes. Well, it was supposed to be twenty, but I got to thirteen and I couldn't wait any more. I opened them a tiny sliver and I saw nothing but a little coffee shop/restaurant, and an empty parking lot, with one car that had to belong to the staff. I opened them a little more and all the kids were asleep, and just like the day I crossed over that doorstep I knew something was very, very wrong.

I closed my eyes again and I listened for those bells and I tried to think about what I could do. I could try to wake up the others, and then what would happen to them? Would it be worse than whatever was going to happen next? Trying to think was like trying to swim through an ice bath; every thought kept freezing up. Could I stumble into the coffee shop and beg them for help? And say what, exactly? I knew how fast Elizabeth and Jessica could turn, their little heads swiveling, their voices honey soft. *Adolescence is so difficult; no, please don't judge her; we just have to be patient with these flights of fancy. I think she's having a really hard day. Mother in prison, you know.*

Then I saw it sticking out from behind the driver's seat. A crinkled CVS bag, and inside it two empty bottles of Benadryl. And then, lying on Jessica's empty seat, were two empty bottles of gin.

The bells tinkled over the doorway.

I shut my eyes and put myself back into a sleeping pose, trying to remember if I'd been leaning against the window or stretched back in my seat. The door opened and I heard two bodies settle back in, and the smell of hot chocolate filled the van.

I tried to just keep breathing, the way I would if I was asleep, and I tried to make my thoughts come to me faster. *Disappear something. Anything*, begged part of my brain, and another part answered back: *And then what?* And another part was furious, skipping right past fear, because on top of everything else they'd done, the Loves knew how much I enjoyed hot chocolate. Topped with whipped cream. I think it was that anger that did it. Because it means I didn't fall apart from what I heard next.

"You ready, babe?" Elizabeth's voice sounded thick and slow.

"Yeah." I think Jessica must have been turning, looking at us. "Will it hurt?"

"No. They're already out. It'll be just like going to sleep in the ocean." And then a window rolled up.

Make them disappear, begged my brain. But that had never worked before. And Jessica's keys had got "lost" so many times that she'd made the car ignition keyless. They wouldn't care now if I took away anything else in the car either, even their hot chocolate they'd just got.

I thought of that hot chocolate, and those gingerbread houses, and all the food we never got to eat, and the bodies sleeping all
around me (or maybe pretending to, just like me.) I thought of
that emptiness, that hollow space inside both of these women.
The one they kept trying to fill with hashtags and stories where
they were the heroes, saving their little rainbow tribe.

And that's when I knew what I wanted to do. Wherever
I'd come from, bright storeroom, mossy bridge, outer space, I
didn't care. If there was any logic or reason, anyone or anything I
could beg. I begged them to let me just do this. I wasn't wishing
away a living thing, not really. Just something that belonged to
them. Something they needed. Not a breaking of the rules. Just
a little wiggly loophole that maybe had always been there.

From one breath to the next, that's how fast it worked.

<hr>

I feel kind of sorry for the EMTs that came squealing into the
parking lot, eleven minutes later, frantic from rushing as fast as
they dared on Highway One. And then just as frantically bend-
ing over the two women's bodies, their skin already turning gray.
The electric paddles thudded over their bodies again and again,
but no response. Of course, there was no hope, never had been,
not thanks to me. But it's not like I was going to tell them.

I don't feel sorry for the sheriffs, though, or the detectives that
pounced on the van full of brown children, all of us drugged and
waiting for the uniforms to come to our rescue. The Benadryl
made everything smeary and far away, and we all kept drifting

even as the cops and then the social workers kept asking their endless questions. We didn't answer them. We knew whose side they'd been on.

At one point I leaned over to Sienna and we took each other's hands. "You can stop counting now," I told her. I was hoping she wouldn't ask me if I had anything to do with what had happened to the Loves. I don't think I could have lied.

Another one I feel kind of sorry for is the coroner. That first one, trying to explain how not one but two women just under forty had dropped dead on a sunny afternoon. Good health, no underlying conditions, nothing in their systems but alcohol. No marks anywhere on their bodies. And then his scalpel prying open their flesh—god, I would give up my power in a second if I could have just been there to see it. Did he scream? Did he swear? Did he run to the phone on the wall or pick up the one in his pocket, shouting something like "you'd better get in here now"? I like to imagine the cameras clicking, eyes growing wide, as they pried open the chest cavity and they found it, the fist-sized thing that showed up in each woman's chest when I made their beating hearts disappear.

Obsidian, the autopsy note said, in a file I stole from one of the reporters. I knew what obsidian was, thanks to the Stephen King book I'd read when I was hiding from the Loves in the library. Heavy and brittle, jagged edges poking into the women's ribs. There were words, too, etched into each one. The coroners would have rinsed off the blood, watching everything they'd ever learned run down the drain with it. And then once the red liquid ran off, they would have held the black hearts up to the light to read it, Jessica and Elizabeth's favorite phrase: "Live, Laugh, Love."

Author's note: This piece is based on the horrendous real-life story of Jennifer and Sarah Hart, two white women who adopted six Black children and then proceeded to abuse them for years. (In a ghoulish twist, they brought their children to Black Lives Matter rallies.) At every turn, the Harts used their whiteness to shield themselves from consequences, even as the children tried many times to get help. Finally, when the Harts feared that they might face some accountability, they drugged their children with Benadryl and then drove their car off of a cliff, killing everyone inside. This story depicts much of that abuse, but with a very different ending. The women in my story get a tiny helping of what the real-life Harts so richly deserved.

The Road out of Nowhere

The car clock read 9:57, and there were no rednecks in the parking lot. Emilio had scoped it out twice before he pulled in for gas, watching the white line of the gauge slip a degree closer to empty. He paid with a $10 and asked the clerk for his change in dimes, and he saw the green eyes flickering over his brown skin, darting out to his Honda with California plates. Emilio was glad he'd scraped every sticker from the bumper, removed every bit of radical literature from view. The clerk made sure their hands never touched.

At the dirty phone booth Emilio slipped the coins through, a string of silver connecting him half a country away, to where Irene picked up, breathless, on the fourth or fifth ring.

"So you a Texan yet?" She had an uncanny ability to know when it was him on the line. He could hear her keys rattling into the dish by the phone, the rustle of what may have been grocery bags plopping onto the floor. He imagined her stepping around the looping yellow cord of the kitchen phone, settling herself at the table, surrounded by the books and newspapers she never let get too far away.

"Ha. I can't wait to be out of here. The 8-track broke in San Antonio and it's been all Merle Haggard and Lord Almighty Radio ever since. Oh, and some fireside chat from Jimmy Carter."

He could hear her snort over the line, and their cat's impudent little "mrrroow," the sound that meant, "I have claimed your lap; there will be no discussion."

"Guess what?" Her voice always got that lilt when it was about to tell you something really good. "They hired back Mariela and the others today. The foreman took one look at the line of people around his office and just said, 'All right, what did I do now?'" He could almost feel her triumphant laughter inside his own chest.

"I knew you could do it. That foreman had better watch his step around you."

So many times in his life Emilio had wished for superpowers: When he was growing up he'd wanted nothing more than a pair of Superman fists whenever his father's rages began. Right now he wanted a pair of magic boots that would cross the hundreds of night miles, the murmuring pines and the cottonwoods, and bring him to Irene in a scant few steps. He would stroke the soft fur of the tabby they'd gleefully named "ProletaryCat," trace his hand over the low hill of Irene's shirt, where the new human inside was forming cell by cell.

"So are you sick of I-10? Which little dot on my road atlas are you?"

So many times Emilio had watched his parents lie to each other without a thought. *The store didn't have that meat on sale today*, was his mom's favorite, her way of covering up for the emptiness of her wallet. *I had to stay late at work*, was his father's. Their path was nothing Emilio wanted to follow. He had never lied to Irene, and he wouldn't now. He let the crackling, staticky line carry the sound of him sucking in his breath.

"I'm not on I-10. I'm on some road called 385."

"Wait, why?" He could almost hear her finger tracing the faint lines folded open in front of her on the table, and hear her voice catch when it stopped. "The only reason to be on that road is Odessa. Tell me that's not where you are now?"

I'm just stopping for a beer after work with the guys. Get off my back, woman! His father had never realized that his family could count the number of beers in his voice.

"I have to at least go and see. He was my best friend." Had been, anyway.

"But, love, Manuel's not buried there. What do you think you might see?"

"I don't know." He could feel his throat threatening to swell, and he made himself let out a long slow breath, counting to four, even though he could practically feel the expensive seconds slipping away. "I just ... I have to at least see where he died. I can't be so close and not go." He slipped the last of his dimes into the slot.

"Emilio. I know what he meant to you, I do. But that's not a place you want to be in the middle of the night, alone, in fucking Texas." As if in response, a pickup sped by, a pair of Confederate flags flapping in the breeze, his chest tightening until it was well out of sight. "Please don't put me in this role, the wife at home in curlers saying please be careful and come home to me."

"You haven't worn curlers since you were sixteen." But the point was made, all the same, hanging on the wire between them, and he knew it. It hung over him even through their uneasy goodbyes, all through the long minutes until he turned off U.S. Route 385 and towards the end of East Blossom Street, the address from the coroner's report buried deep in a folder in Manuel's parents' garage.

Emilio had never even seen a picture of the Crazy Horse bar, but for more than four years it had loomed huge and neon-bright in his imagination. In his mind it was always festering with rusted redneck trucks in the parking lot, thick oil stains shimmering like blood in the light of the streetlamps, bands of roving white men sprawled across their cars and tossing glittering bottles at their feet.

The place he pulled up to now was shuttered and dark, a "For Sale" sign hanging loose and faded from the door and a "No Trespassing" sign on the driveway chain. A station wagon on blocks rusted away in a corner and weeds pushed their way through the asphalt. No sign with the name of the bar, no wooden Indian glowering above the front door. No trace, however faint, of the friend who had died in this parking lot, this friend who had always reminded Emilio of a stray cat. Covered with scars, quick to show his claws, but secretly wanting a warm patch of sun and sometimes a soft place to land. The sad thing was, Manuel hated cats. Weak, he had always called them.

There wasn't a drop of light anywhere except for his own headlights, and the blackness seemed to grow thicker towards the back of the lot. Emilio didn't know what kind of answers he might have found in this place, but there was nothing here except faint scrabbling sounds, maybe jackrabbits, and in the trees what sounded like crows, the branches shivering in the dark.

What was he doing in a place like this? This was the stuff of *The Twilight Zone,* of mournful ballads sung to a strumming guitar: *And that was the last anyone heard/From Emilio Cruz* ... Back in the little house on Ygnacio, Irene would be covering the table with leaflets and articles and piles of books under the terrible wincing light of the kitchen lamp, while inside her the cells were dividing and dividing, walls building themselves. He imagined himself in five months or so, sneaking into the nursery to hear his child's sleeping breaths, summoning all his tenderness into a single finger stroking a tiny brow. He didn't belong here. It was time to go home.

Emilio's mother had always welcomed her son's friends, feeding Manuel and letting him crash on their couch without asking why. On each boy's 18th birthday she'd given them a

St. Christopher's medal on a looping gold chain. "To guide you safely on your journeys," she'd said. Ha. Emilio wondered where Manuel's necklace was now. Was it nestled inside tissue paper in Manuel's old bedroom? Had a drunken fist pulled it from Manuel's neck, leaving it to be trampled into the ground where Emilio now stood? He leaned down to a patch of smooth dirt by the No Trespassing sign and slipped his own medal off his neck, fingers catching the tiny dent on the back, the slim gold chain with a knot he'd never been able to untie. He didn't know what words to say here. If he were Manuel, he would have poured a bottle of liquor out onto the ground—even if that meant stealing the bottle first—and then gone around looking for someone to fight. And where had that kind of thinking led his friend? Emilio was standing at the end of that road. He had no idea which part of this place had held Manuel's last breaths, which piece of ground had been cursed. Had he stood over it already? This was Texas, the land stolen and passed back and forth like a bloody smallpox blanket. Maybe this whole place was cursed.

He turned to walk back to the waiting car, and he stumbled over a wide crack in the asphalt, a crack he could have sworn he hadn't seen before. When he stood up, beads of red were spreading in two thin lines across his palms. His steps, faster now, echoed into the dark.

He started up the Honda and slid open the radio dial, filling the car with a preacher's voice railing about yet another imagined threat to the nuclear family. Huh. When Emilio was growing up, so much of the damage came from inside the family itself. His father's fury at heading up a household of seven with a paycheck barely enough for three, swollen with the tears he never let himself cry, all of it festering inside, a black hole that spread past his father and tried to eat through all of them in turn.

The air inside the car was stifling and he slid down the window for the night breeze, fumbled at the radio again until Freddy Fender was singing "You Can't Get Here from There," his voice slowly fading into range. The map showed Emilio the way he should go; he had maybe five or ten minutes along a splinter of road that led back to I-10 and then several hours more to El Paso and the long way back to the life he had built.

Emilio could faintly see the long ribbon of the highway ahead, a streak of black lit up with the flash of headlights, when in front of him loomed what felt like the only red light for miles, a single bulb dangling in the dark. He sighed and brought the car to a stop; his brown skin might as well be a red cape to any policeman lurking in the shadows. Next to the metal pole was a diner closed up for the night. And a slim figure leaning against the wall, lit by a single overhead light buzzing with moths. In the arch of light over the pale head nothing could be seen except black clothes and the brim of a cowboy hat, and then the figure stepped out of the circle and fixed his gaze on the windshield.

Yellow light splashed against the clothes, coated in what looked to be a layer of dust. The man emerged from the light and leaned a pale face into the passenger side window and Emilio's hands flicked the radio off and cranked the window down. *What are you doing?* He wanted to ask his hands. The man's eyes were like a rabbit's, red-rimmed and pale.

"Really appreciate your stopping by, friend. It's awful lonely out here. Mind if I ask where you're headed? I could sure use a ride." The eyes were rimmed with circles that looked nearly etched in, like he couldn't even remember the last time he'd slept.

I'm so sorry, I can't pick up hitchhikers. My wife won't let me, you know how it is. It's what he'd practiced just in case this came up, he and Irene rolling their eyes at the idea of either of them "letting" the other do anything.

"I'm going home to Oakland but, um, I'm staying with friends in El Paso for the night." Yeah, that sounded like what he'd practiced.

"That's a mighty long drive for one person." The voice was reedy and thin, and the face leaning into the window was still draped in shadows.

"Yeah, I was supposed to drive back with someone else but that fell through, and if I'm not back at work Monday morning they'll fire me."

His mouth was full-on betraying him now. Or was it his brain? He stared at his feet as if they might also suddenly grow minds of their own and speed him off into the darkness somewhere. Or him and the stranger both, because the man was reaching for the passenger door and Emilio's hands were unlocking it. The man slid onto the seat and the light flashed green and the passenger door slammed shut.

As the road hummed underneath them the stranger stuck a pink hand into the air, faint with the smell of tobacco. As he shook Emilio's hand he seemed to be saying something, like a name—Dave? Gabe? Then he lit a cigarette without asking, without offering one.

"So, friend, what brings you to Texas?" There was something wrong with his voice. It sounded like it was coming through a long tunnel. Long and cold and dark. But he was sitting right there.

I went to my cousin's wedding. I was one of the groomsmen. He'd practiced this too.

"Well, did you ever read about the cops in Houston who killed José Enriquez?"

Yeah, that sounded like a cousin's wedding story, all right.

"Can't say that I have. Sounds like a sad one."

And then the words began to unspool from Emilio as if the stranger were pulling them out, a tale sewn together from news articles, court transcripts, testimonials that had followed one after the other. The last hours in the life of twenty-three-year-old José, drunk and belligerent at a nightclub until someone called the cops, who came thundering out of their cars to beat him bloody, not forgetting to arrest him before they were done. The battered body being dragged into the jail, looking hideous enough that the desk sergeant ordered the cops to take their victim to the hospital. José never made it there. He was found floating in the bayou three days later.

"Well, that surely sounds awful." The drawl echoed in the chilly car.

"They had a trial. They convicted the cops. The jury gave them a fine. One dollar." There'd been marches, days of them, throngs of people with dollar bills pinned to themselves.

"So my comrades and I went there and helped organize a people's trial." Dozens and dozens of testimonies over four days; some telling José's story, some telling their own, of humiliations and beatings and worse. Emilio had been translating, so his mouth had to form each painful word, so many of them calling up memories he had tied up and stashed neatly away. And all the while he had to sit calm in the little folding chair, letting the microphones echo and whine.

The stranger was utterly still, nothing but a plume of smoke rising from the glowing red tip of the cigarette.

"Well, that sounds awful too. Must make you mighty angry."

"You have no idea." What a smart thing to admit to a strange white man on a deserted road in the middle of the night.

Now the tobacco-stained fingers spun at the radio and it hummed into life. Where nothing but Hank Williams and preaching had been, something else now sang from the speakers. Voices crooned low and threatened to crack. A guitar strummed in the dark. *In the pines, in the pines*, a low voice sang: *where the sun don't ever shine/I would shiver the whole night through*

... And as if the stranger had called forth the song and the song had called forth the cold, the car grew chilly. Speeding along, darkness all around.

"So, if you don't mind my asking, friend, why were you passing through Odessa? It's mighty far out of your way."

"My wife said the same thing." Emilio grabbed at his throat for the looping gold chain, nails grazing skin before he remembered where the medal was now.

"I had this friend. Manuel Torres. We were born the same month. We grew up together, three streets apart." Two lanky kids thrumming with anger like a live wire, each of them ready with fists to defend the other. Like shadows of each other, in so many ways. The differences were tiny enough at first—always a lunch in Emilio's bag, even when it was a roll of old tortillas and a smear of beans, but some days nothing at all in Manuel's—but they had widened and widened over the years.

"He was smarter than I was, but he ... if you'd met his family you'd understand. I graduated high school and went to college, and he dropped out and went into the Army. He came to see me get my diploma and a week later he was on a plane to boot camp. Manuel always had one foot in two different kinds of life. But so did I. If I'd stayed there ..." Silence from the seat next to him. As if the stranger were a red-eyed smoking priest and the car a confessional. Back to those stuffy mornings in church, his mother wincing as she knelt on sore knees, all those years scrubbing floors in hotels. The bruises flowering out of her shirt.

"Everyone told me not to go to San Francisco. All those hippies and radicals. And my first year on campus was the Third World strike and who did I meet but a bunch of actual revolutionaries. For the first time, I felt like my life had a purpose. Manuel, though, he laughed his ass off when I told him I'd become a communist." The dark rolled along. The smoke filled the car. He and Manuel, both of them with one foot on each side of a furrowing gap in the road. And the years pouring in, pulling that gap apart, the two of them standing on opposite sides, staring at each other. And then the furrow reaching out and pulling Manuel down into it forever. The words kept coming, these heavy things Emilio spent so much time keeping inside his chest, that he had no business saying to this stranger, in this place.

"He was coming home from Vietnam. He got off the Greyhound in Odessa. Maybe he was going to stop and get drunk, catch the next bus later. Maybe he met a woman; I don't know. But he got into a fight in a bar. I can't see him starting anything when he was days from home. And if someone was provoking him, he would have warned them plenty." Again that stray cat, hissing and showing its claws before finally drawing blood.

"I don't know who had the knife. What I do know is, it wasn't his wounds that killed him. I mean, not exactly. He might have lived if someone had called an ambulance. But they just left him in the parking lot to die."

"Like that boy in Houston."

"Like that boy in Houston. Yes." The anger was heating up now, the way it had always simmered inside his father, inside Manuel, inside his own younger self. Pouring out of his fists, sometimes before he even knew who he was angry at, and why. José Enriquez, Manuel Torres, everyone who looked like them; the price for their lives and the wages for an hour in the fields picking lettuce: exactly the same. The tears blurred the empty road in front of him. He wondered, if he took his hands off the wheel, would the car stay on this path, stabbing straight ahead in the dark?

"So you thought you'd, what? Go there and see if you could learn anything?"

Sure. At ten at night, he'd have found a lot of people interested in answering the questions of some greaser with California plates.

"Confront them, maybe?" Emilio's head rang with the truth of it. He'd been lying to himself. Irene had sensed that from fifteen hundred miles away. The stranger had sensed it after ... how long had they been driving now? He couldn't remember the last time he'd seen a light on the road, or a car in either direction. They might have been the only two people in the world, the rest of the world fallen away, and they would never know it, would just keep driving on into the night, dawn never coming.

"What bar did you say this was?"

Of all the things not to tell this stranger—what had he said his name was again? Dave? Gabe? Wayne?—this should have stuck

Emilio's lips together the hardest. What he needed to do right then was turn the volume way up and let the haunted voice sing about shivering the whole night through.

"Manuel died in the parking lot of the Crazy Horse bar. The only thing in hundreds of miles named after a Native American and it's a fucking bar." Full of men, swollen with beer, looking at a skinny brown kid as something flickering between predator and prey. Or a grease spot under their shoes. How many of those men were clogging up bars, board rooms, factory floors, every day? It hurt to imagine it.

"So you went there and found what?"

"Nothing." Emilio's hands trembled in the chill. "An empty lot."

"Well, my friend, I think you must have gone to the wrong place. Maybe you were lost. The Crazy Horse is still there. Definitely one of them kicker bars."

"One of those what?" Emilio imagined a row of cowboy boots, their pointed toes aimed at ribs, a jaw, a collarbone.

"Yeah. Short for shitkicker. Um … everyone works on a ranch has shit all over their boots. It's one of them bars with everyone's name practically painted on the barstools. Probably some of the same old regulars as was there when your friend … was there."

The low voice rattled the speakers. "*I'm going … where the cold wind blows.*" Emilio could see his breath curling into the air. He knocked at the heater and the knob spun, useless and quiet.

"Take us back and I'll show you just where it is."

And the stranger pulled something long and knotted from his boot. It was a St. Christopher's medal. The travelers' patron saint.

"You can borrow this. For luck." There was no light in the car, but the medal gave off a flash of bright gold. There was something Emilio was supposed to know about this necklace, he was sure of it. He tried to remember what it was. But now his foot was lifting off the gas pedal, just as the story had spooled from Emilio without warning, just as his hands had opened the door while he watched. Now the car was shuddering down into each lower gear, and then the wheels spun around and back to Odessa, back to where his friend's life had spilled out onto the ground.

The car was utterly silent now. Even the singing voice had gone quiet. The stranger pointed down one road or another, directing Emilio where to go, often at the last second, barely enough time to make each turn. Emilio didn't recognize anything, but then the stranger had said he must have been lost before. In the silence he could imagine it, all of it, the once-dead lights of the parking lot now gleaming and blocking out the light of the stars, a neon Indian inexplicably grinning and cracking an endless whip again and again, saloon doors swinging wide and letting everyone in. Himself, thundering into the bar and demanding words with the men who had stabbed his friend. The images were flickering on the back of his eyelids, as if someone had started up an old movie in a dark room. Like an old Western, except this time the bad guys and the good guys had finally switched. The soundtrack a ballad, the singer's voice building full and low as it swung towards the climax. *And thus began the revenge of Emilio Cruz…*

And then the Crazy Horse was looming ahead, at the dead end of East Blossom Street. The movie in the dark room was playing loud and bright now: the door slamming open, the sneering men in shit-stained shoes. There would always be men like them; there would always be cops using black and brown bodies for sport and judges that would slap at their wrists with a bloody dollar bill. There would always be foremen like the ones at Irene's factory, who liked to corner women in his office to "talk about their future" and fire them if they spoke up. All his struggles, all of Irene's, their comrades', and for every powerful figure they beat back there were two more sprouting like weeds from rotten ground.

Faint as the radio in the back of his brain was a low voice in a tone like a warning, but it was drowned out by the sound of the car's tires pulling up to the edge of the lot. The stranger opened thin dry lips into a smile and settled the necklace into Emilio's palm.

"Glad to help out, friend. Sometimes a man just knows what he has to do."

As Emilio's hand slammed the door shut, he heard it again, now crackling in his brain like static, but over it the imagined guitars were strumming and the voice was singing out clear: *Emilio strode up to the doorway/revenge on his mind …* The cars in this lot were practically glowing, they were so bright, and, just as he had pictured it, the neon Indian grinned and cracked a whip again and again. The stranger leaned on the Honda, tipping his hat. Emilio's hand slid up as if to tip an imaginary one of his own, a gesture he'd never made in his life, and as he did so the necklace slid out of his hand and onto the asphalt.

The slim gold chain with a stubborn thick knot, and at the end a St. Christopher's medal. With a tiny dent on the back. The one he'd left in an empty lot, in the dirt by the No Trespassing sign.

If there'd been a red light inside his head it would have been firing up, ready to blare in alarm if he crossed the threshold lit up impossibly bright, if he crossed over that bloody ground. Was it hungry, the land, for more blood to drink? He was thinking in slow motion, staring at the necklace, the dent, the knot, its glow coming from nowhere, the lights glowing off the cars, coming from nowhere too. This place was a bright glowing nowhere luring him in, and the stranger had pulled his fury out of him, spun it into a song of revenge. "Must make you mighty angry." Emilio's head beat with it. His hands had formed into fists, shapes he'd long since trained himself not to form.

In the lot in front of him it was as if the film reel had slipped, as if the song were caught between two radio stations. One layer was the empty lot, the No Trespassing sign, a place he knew to stay away from, the ballad a warning, cued up to the next verse; the other was lit up in technicolor and neon, white teeth grinning, the ballad a call, cued up to the next verse. His tears blurred his vision. Superimposed on each other, the edges blurring where they touched, and himself at the center of it, seeing both, two versions of now, two versions of what would come next. Two movie reels laying over each other, both real. *Lying* over, he reminded himself. And in his head Manuel began to laugh, at such narrow prissiness, but really the laughter came from fear. Fear of that widening gap.

It was that, then, that sent Emilio to his knees, his hands opening and bracing him against the cracked asphalt. And now the dueling songs quieted as he spoke.

"I'm sorry, man. I'm so sorry. I know if this were the other way around, I know what you would have done. But I can't do that stuff anymore." He stopped. No lying, even to the air.

"That's not true. I can. But I'm not going to. Look, I'll never know who you would have been if you'd found your way home. I do know you deserved a better world than one that let you bleed to death on the road out of nowhere. And I can't fight for that world if I go back now." There would always be cops doing target practice, foremen cornering women in their offices, bent backs picking lettuce and sore knees scrubbing floors.

And now his chest was almost caved in with the sorrow, like all his life he'd been made of soft clay and the God he didn't believe in had reached in a thumb and smudged right through it.

"I know you'd make fun of me if you saw me right now. But only because you were terrified of a crying man. It's like a prison, living like that. I know that prison. My dad was in it my whole life. He never got to leave it. Neither did you."

He doubled over and a few of his tears fell on the cursed ground, and in that second he heard a pair of boot heels turning around, their steps growing fainter and fainter. The rhythm sounded almost defeated, almost sad. Emilio held himself perfectly still, not turning to look, barely breathing until the sound of the steps disappeared into the darkness back towards Odessa. And again there was nothing here but what sounded like jackrabbits, and in the trees what sounded like crows, and, much closer, the beating of his own heart.

Emilio laid the medal back in the dirt in the middle of nowhere, at the base of a telephone pole. There was nothing to distinguish this from the thousands of poles he had passed on the way here, the thousands he would pass on the way back home. Nothing except a secret only he would know. Nothing to mark the moment he chose, again, what he was carrying with him, and what he was leaving behind.

Author's note: The police killing in this story is very heavily based on the real-life story of the police killing of José Campos Torres in Houston in 1977.

Huitzol and the Rope of Thorns

He wasn't speeding. Roberto knew he wasn't speeding, but he also knew that didn't matter once the headlights began flashing behind him. "Pull over," commanded the car, the one that had been following behind for at least a mile. Ever since Waze detoured him away from a backup on 24 and into a warren of streets with names like Black Forest Court and Meadow View Circle.

He'd gone to one of those Know Your Rights trainings once, those things that always smelled to him of patchouli and naivete. *Never pull over on a deserted road*, had been one of the first warnings. *Find a place with witnesses.* Really easy to follow that advice now when his car's GPS showed nothing but Crest View Drives all around.

"Pull over," the speaker crackled again. Now he saw something in the rearview mirror, a hand movement from the passenger seat. Calling for backup, maybe, the tones crackling through the air: "Male Hispanic, tattoos on arms, evading pursuit." Turning him into something disposable, something dangerous. The siren started up its high-pitched wail. After sirens came doors snapping open, pink hands pulling out billy clubs. The scars on his arms remembered.

Roberto pulled into a wide spot in the road, just before something called Blackberry Lane, and they stopped behind him, pinning him in. He turned off the engine and they were already coming, dirt crunching under their feet. He picked up his phone but his sweaty hands dropped it, and it slid under the passenger seat. No retrieving it now: His hands had to stay in plain view. Not that that would protect him.

A face leaned into his window, pale blond hair in a buzz cut, eyes dark as a bruise. Another at the passenger side, this face slightly rounder, an auburn mustache spreading over his lip.

"What brings you out here tonight?" asked the güero, the one at Roberto's left shoulder.

This was like one of those Choose Your Own Adventure books Roberto had loved as a kid. *If you remember what they told you in the workshop, and say you don't need to answer their questions, turn to page 11. If you answer the question, because you're alone and afraid, turn to page 20.*

"I'm a writer. I had a book event tonight."

Their eyes snaked over Roberto's tattoos: an Easter lily that had begun its life as a dagger, and the butterflies that had been bullets once. They couldn't see the only one left untouched, the one stretching over Roberto's chest. "Don't Start No Shit, Won't Be No Shit," in black ink fading to blue.

"Sure you did," Güero said.

If you let him decide you're lying, then turn to page 17, where he will ask you for your ID. If you show him your books as proof, turn to page 22, where they will see the illustration on the cover and you'll be lucky if all they do is ask for ID.

"License and registration, please."

If you comply and reach for your registration, turn to page 34. If you ask them to please not shoot you while you're reaching for your registration, turn to page 32. If you tell them you don't need to show them anything, because you haven't done anything wrong, turn to page 48. The ending would be the same on any page.

Behind him on the back seat was an open box, holding a half-dozen copies of a book with an ending that was entirely different. *Huitzol and the Rope of Thorns,* Book Five in a series of graphic novels about private detective-turned-avenger Luís Montoya, and his sidekick Huitzol, the terrifying and vindictive god of war. Huitzol, who served as Detective Montoya's personal assassin, dispatching his victims before returning to his spirit world, leaving no trace.

There was not, as far as Roberto knew, an actual god called Huitzol. Roberto had invented him, sewn together from bits of deities from indigenous groups all over Mexico, just like Roberto himself. And Roberto still had to find out which page his life would turn to.

"Right away, officer. Excuse me; my wallet's in my sweatshirt pocket." And Roberto turned his hands into pincers, nothing that could possibly grip a gun. He opened the glove compartment using that same pincer hand, and the sound of the opening latch rang out in his head like a shot.

Redhead walked off with the license, and Roberto could feel the net pull around him, tight and invisible. But his license was clean, because he'd made sure it was, and so was his car. The disappointment practically radiated from both of the cops: the anticipated click of those cuffs, his prone body slamming into their car.

"You say you're some kind of writer?" Redhead asked as he handed back Roberto's license, his voice thick with distaste.

"Yes, sir."

"Those your books there?" Güero took a copy of Book Five and handed one to Redhead. Roberto could see on both of their faces the moment they realized what they were looking at.

Huitzol's eyes glared up from the cover, perfectly round and jet black. A thorned rope stretched out from his side, thick with the flesh of his victims: two cops, the rope slicing open their uniforms, their blood flowing onto the ground.

Huitzol had only one kind of victim, because Detective Montoya took only one kind of client: someone who'd lost a loved one to the cops and had spent years fighting for justice, to no result. Nobody else to turn to but Huitzol. The perfect assassin who came alive only when needed, occupying whatever mask or figurine was nearby. For this book, Huitzol's favorite form had been a puppet with a lacquered paper body and the round head of a coconut shell, black eyes huge and perfectly round in his painted white face.

"You like to write this sick shit?" Güero pointed to a page in the middle, Huitzol looming over a terrified cop, the rope poised to crack like a whip.

If you know that there is no right answer, stay perfectly still and wait to see if you will survive the next few minutes. Roberto had first dreamed up Huitzol from the hospital room where he lay recovering from an encounter with Oakland PD and some billy clubs. The same kinds of clubs now swinging from the waistbands of both of these men, even if their badges showed they represented Orinda. Roberto could actually smell the fear seeping out of his pores, and he knew they could too.

Güero cast a glance at his partner, a secret handshake, and Roberto's stomach curled in on itself. With a quick twist of his hand Güero flicked his body camera to "off," and as if in a call and response Redhead did the same. Güero then strolled over to the car and reached for the camera on the dashboard, and a tiny red light disappeared. Roberto's hands practically itched to pull out his phone, start recording. But he could see the police report now: *Suspect appeared to reach for a weapon under his seat.* He knew full well the voodoo magic of police reports that could render any object into a gun.

"The hell is this thing?" Güero pulled a paper mache puppet off the rearview mirror, a miniature version of Huitzol's form in Book Five.

"My daughter made that for me. It's delicate." Lucy had sent it from Mexico City, where she was studying design.

"What are you smuggling in here?" Güero pulled an actual switchblade from his hip, as if to slice open the belly of the god, rib to rib. Roberto wondered if they would plant that knife on his body and then turn their cameras back on.

Redhead was reading from the book's intro now: "To summon Huitzol"—only he pronounced it "Hoo-it-zole"—"you call him three times and with all proper respect."

Redhead's entire voice was a sneer. "Like Candyman? Hoo-it-zole, hoo-it-zole, hoo-it-zole?"

Roberto actually found himself searching the night sky for signs of a god, a god who didn't exist. The night sky, of course, did not respond. The air lay still, nothing there but the three of them and the houses at the end of long driveways, quiet and dark. Redhead tossed the puppet into a patch of mud at the side of the road.

"Step out of the car, please," Güero practically grinned. For Book Five, Roberto had researched how many people had been killed while already handcuffed, and the number had sent him to the restroom to puke. He raised himself out of the car, hands open wide. Güero reached for his glittering cuffs, and Redhead pulled the billy club away from his waist, black and shining.

To throw this story away and change the ending entirely, you know what to do.

Roberto's voice was so soft he could barely hear it himself. "Who's here? It's Roberto. Who's here? I need you. Who's here? It's 9:59." If the cops had bothered to read further, they would know that this was how to summon the god of war and revenge. The god that Roberto was summoning now, a ridiculous thing to do for a god that Roberto himself had brought onto the page.

For a breath there was nothing, only a skittering of leaves against the asphalt, like the rattling of dry bones. But then the air slowed to a halt, growing warm, growing thick.

And then he came rushing in. Out of the patch of muck where he'd been thrown. Black eyes perfectly round in his white painted face, his limbs dipping up and down, his black mouth a grimace, a Punch without Judy, a jittering thing. Güero's mouth fell open as he gasped, but Redhead never even got a chance to turn around.

The god's little hands were draped in a long rope of thorns, one that seemed to grow out of the ground and down from the oak trees overhead. The rope wrapped first around Güero, around his open mouth, and the thorns held his tongue very still. Then the rope lashed him and Redhead back to back, thorns tearing at their uniforms, wrapping nearly everything but their eyes, wide and terrified.

Huitzol was light and deadly, sailing through the air and leaping from one place to another without seeming to move. Just as Roberto had drawn him to be. Now the god's little hands split open a knothole in the oak tree behind them, and the knothole glowed red like the tip of a cigarette. Then he pulled the knothole down to the base of the tree, the trunk a narrow glowing mouth. And then the hands of the god reached for the bundle and pulled it into the red.

Roberto couldn't make himself look. The muffled screams were enough. When he opened his eyes, Huitzol was smiling and the tree was back to itself, but a faint column of smoke rose from the bark. Roberto felt for shame and there was nothing there. Only smoke whispering onto the night air and the quiet descending again all around.

Nobody came out of the houses high up on the hill; no lights flickered on. A Tesla roared around the corner just then, not even slowing at the cop car with no cops in it, or the brown-skinned man staring at a tree that curled over the road.

"That's great, asshole." Roberto knew that this was probably the wrong thing to say in this situation, but was there a right thing?

"Now when those two cops go missing, they'll track where their cell phones were last, and they'll track the last license plate they looked up, and I'll be the last one to fucking see them alive." There was also no time for Roberto to take a second and reorder his entire conception of the world. One that now involved a god that he'd apparently invented from fury and Black Magic ink.

Huitzol opened his mouth and words came out. His voice was high and thin, just the way a god made of paper would sound. And the words were a tangle of languages Roberto could barely recognize, much less speak. It felt like standing under a tall growing thing with the spindly needles of a mountain pine, the fruit of a coconut, and the gnarled base of a ceiba tree. This was just what Roberto deserved, having made this god by borrowing from the Huichol and the Nahua and the Maya (and a bit of Toltec thrown in, only because the Toltecs were cool.) He shook his head at the puppet, and Huitzol leapt through the car's open window and into the messy back seat where a copy of Book Two rested against the floor. The lacquered hands pointed to Chapter Nineteen: the fate of a trio of aged Klansmen who'd escaped consequences since 1982, until Detective Montoya tracked them down. And the god's mouth stretched wide in a grin.

Roberto had loved scary stories from the time he was little, and his favorite stories came from his grandmother, who'd grown up in swampy East Texas. There were dangerous creatures living in the dark swamps, she told him, who liked to snatch up wayward children and leave behind a changeling, a twin. The changelings could barely walk, barely talk, and they fell dead within a few days. It was where he'd first got the idea for the fate of the trio of Klansmen in Book Two, their changelings formed from the swollen limbs of a mangrove tree.

Huitzol had conjured up a pair of changelings from the cops' own billy clubs, while the smoke rose from the bark of their grave. Roberto had watched the black metal grow pale and soft, watched it sprout hair and teeth and fingernails. But he couldn't make himself watch their horrible sick lumbering, the hands grasping into the air. He'd watched them grow smaller in the rearview mirror, making himself breathe in, breathe out, the whole drive home. He'd passed out fully clothed on his bed, under a shelf full of pothos plants, his sleep shallow and weak. In his dreams the dangling vines grew thorns, thick with blood and strips of pink flesh.

The last time he'd survived an encounter with the cops, he'd at least been able to tell someone. He'd even done research before ever starting Book One, interviewing a group of families who had lost someone to the police, feeling hideously guilty that he'd survived while their loved ones hadn't. This time the secret had to stay deeply buried, like the beating of a hideous heart. Worse, he still had to work. The private investigator world was flooded and jobs were hard to come by, especially when you looked like Roberto. So he had to sit at his computer the next morning, scrolling through tax records and financial disclosure forms, the text blurring and sharpening, blurring again, in front of his bloodshot eyes.

Even worse, Huitzol was still not gone. In the books he had disappeared right after dispatching his victims, leaving his old form empty and still. But now he had apparently decided that Roberto's home was his to explore. First his face lit up with the glow of Roberto's laptop, which Roberto pressed firmly shut. "That's off limits. I make my living with that machine." The god blinked and then landed on the shelf of Roberto's orchids, his hands actually gentle as he stroked the petals, the fuchsia and white. Then he discovered the bookshelves, flipping open page after page, leaving the books face down on the rug for Roberto to clean up. Of course. A god wouldn't bother himself with housekeeping. His favorites seemed to be Victor LaValle and

H.P. Lovecraft, but of course the black eyes widened at Mary Shelley's *Frankenstein*. Roberto tried to interest Huitzol in a copy of *Gulliver's Travels*, but the papery hands tossed the book behind the couch.

Next was the television, the boxes of DVDs stacked underneath. While Roberto was gathering up the mess, the TV began blaring the credits to *Monkey Shines*.

"Huitzol! Turn that off." The screen went black and Roberto began to return the books where they belonged. But then he turned and Huitzol was sitting on the couch, starting up Roberto's copy of *Deadly Friend*. He blinked at Roberto as if to say, "You didn't tell me to turn off *all* the movies."

"Jesus. Fine. Huitzol, you are mine to command." The phrase, straight from the books, sounded sour and musty to Roberto's semi-anarchist ears, but it was clear he had to start using it. Huitzol sat up tall (it looked ridiculous on a three-inch-high puppet) as if he'd been waiting for this.

"First of all, Huitzol, don't touch anything in this house if I don't command it." And then Huitzol hovered in the air like a hummingbird, touching nothing at all, eyes on the TV screen.

The lesson went on, like a perverse game of Simon Says, with Roberto telling Huitzol (or thinking at him) phrases like "turn off the TV," and the impish eyes blinking, waiting until Roberto used the magic words, "Huitzol, I command you." Then Huitzol would issue a series of grumbling sounds and turn it off, knowing the screen had to stay dark until the command said otherwise. When that worked well enough, Roberto let Huitzol sit back on the couch, watching his way through a stack of Wes Craven films.

That night, Monday night, Roberto dreamed again of the thorns, growing down from the walls now and reaching out for his face. The doubt blossomed in his chest as he stumbled awake, and any time he closed his eyes he imagined them, the cops and the shuffling things wearing their faces. Where were they now, his walking alibis? Why had no one found them yet? Sooner or later someone would begin to put the pieces together, and when they did Roberto's name would be at the end of that trail. Or at the end of that Blackberry Lane.

The next afternoon it finally came, the knock on his iron screen door. He peeked through his blinds to see the shadow moving, the shape of a long arm, at its end a round fist. A black-and-white cop car stood at the curb, the Orinda logo on its side.

"Mr. Salas?" He had never heard this voice before, he was sure. What was clutched inside that shadowy fist? Maybe a warrant, full of details cherry-picked and damning: the most violent excerpts from Roberto's books, his driver's license as the very last that the two cops had pulled. Possibly even the contents of their body-cam footage; with Roberto's luck, it hadn't been obliterated along with the cops but had saved itself to a cloud somewhere.

He heard his name again, but this time it was clear that there was only one voice, only one shadow stretching over the porch. Roberto breathed in through the second knock, breathed out through the third. And then a beat of silence, and a single set of boots thumped down the steps.

He opened the door to a white business card, tucked into the patched metal screen. An Officer Fuentes asked Roberto to call at his earliest opportunity. He had escaped whatever they had in mind, this time. It had been just a rookie on shit duty this time, leaving only a phone number behind. But next there would surely be more.

Where the hell were the changelings? Had they been found or not? "Send those things home," he'd commanded Huitzol. But had Huitzol even known where those cops lived? Roberto could picture any number of places the changelings might be now, Huitzol's blink essentially saying, "You didn't say *whose* home." Were the conjured bodies rotting somewhere in the desert of Nevada, or floating somewhere in the bay? What was Roberto going to do: drive along every Lane and Court, calling out their names?

Oh, fuck. And where was Huitzol?

"Had to become a writer, didn't you?" Roberto muttered to himself as he surveyed the damage at the end of the block. "Couldn't be a nice boring accountant, like your mom wanted, no sir." He'd failed, thankfully, at being a petty criminal and a wannabe gangster. That was a path that a mentorship and a notebook had pulled him away from, and that he'd fully abandoned the second Lucy was placed in his arms. The notebooks had led to a journalism degree and then a P.I. certificate, and those were all well and good, but they'd also led him here, hadn't they? To a god he'd invented and then brought into the world. And a god that had decided to slip into an Orinda cop car and tie the officer's shoelaces together, sending his car into a telephone pole.

"Huitzol, you could have killed him. That is not okay." Roberto scolded, once they got back inside. This would've sounded more convincing if a tiny part of Roberto wasn't smirking, imagining the bewildered cop trying to explain this one at headquarters.

Huitzol gestured to a copy of Book Five, as if to ask permission to sit on it, which Roberto gave, but then the little hands gestured at the bloody thorns.

"This is different. Those cops in Orinda? They were going to kill me." *And the one from today wasn't going to try to do the same thing? Just a bunch more steps, more official-like?* Roberto shoved the thought beneath the floorboards, where it thumped anyway.

The little god pointed to the desk behind him, to the stack of Book Six drawings showing murderous cops in all stages of death. His round eyes blinked again, and Roberto couldn't explain that those were just books, just wishes and daydreams on paper. Not reality. Because here Huitzol was, as real as the bruised Orinda policeman at the end of the block.

More thoughts thumped at the floor. What if those Orinda cops came back with a warrant, and Huitzol was still this wild and out of control? And even if he wasn't? Roberto had come a long way from the angry kid tattooing bullets onto his arm, but he knew they were still there, just underneath the butterfly wings.

Roberto looked at the perfectly round eyes, the ones Lucy had painted by hand. "That's not what you did in the b—that is not who I wrote you to be. And if you want to stay here, that's who you'll have to be."

The little god sagged, just a little, either chastened or doing a good job of pretending.

Roberto let himself finally collapse in his chair and fumbled for his pink water bottle (another present from Lucy.) As he gulped it down a plan began forming, shiny and clear.

⸻ ◆ ⸻

Blinds drawn, curtains closed, Roberto taught himself how to translate his commands to Huitzol-speak. "Don't touch anything in this house" had to be clarified: "Don't touch anything inside or outside of the house, not without my command." Roberto learned to say, "Close the curtains, but do not swing from them," and "Did I say you could take the form of my Freddy Krueger or Jade Daniels dolls? No. You take only the forms I command." Huitzol actually stuck out what looked like a paper tongue, but he obeyed. Every time Roberto looked through the blinds, there were the same cars at the curb, the same begonias and garden gnomes on his porch. The cops did not come.

When Huitzol had finally learned all of his lessons as paper mache, Roberto let him choose any form he wanted to occupy. He kind of wanted Huitzol to emulate Book Three, where he'd been a tiny pair of hummingbird earrings, poison-tipped and nearly invisible. But then Roberto's Jade Daniels figure sailed into view, the tiny scythe cutting through the air with sheer glee.

It was just after two, Thursday morning. The street was quiet and dark. The streetlights were burning and a dog on the corner was barking and then all of them began howling in turn. Roberto pulled up the blinds and stared at the end of the block, to a patch of darkness under a broken street lamp. And then out of that darkness came two stumbling things in cop uniforms, making their way to his home. In his dreams they had looked nearly human except for their eyes, perfectly round and jet black. Except for the handcuffs sprouting from their wrists, the metal dripping with blood, the cuffs opening and closing like claws. These things shuffling down the street looked just like cops, nothing more, nothing more or less dangerous.

"Well done, Huitzol." This was the god's final test. Roberto's heart lurched as he watched the things approach ever closer, and then he turned and gave Huitzol a command. The little god blinked in confusion but he moved his hands like a conductor's, and the things meant to be cops stopped walking and began a crazed puppet dance. Any second now a neighbor would look through their curtains and see, and this hadn't been part of the plan, but Roberto couldn't stop watching those hands that had been ready to end his life, now jerking through the air with no rhythm, no power to stop.

Then he felt a very light tap on his shoulder, and he sighed and turned to Huitzol. "Okay. Are you ready?" The god nodded and Roberto opened a window and Huitzol flew into the street, where he started up a Mustang that had sat abandoned for weeks. The god's creations obediently lumbered up to the car and without hesitating smashed the windows and pulled up the locks. The thing meant to be Güero folded itself behind the steering wheel and began to maneuver the car, jerking like a marionette. Roberto told Huitzol where to send the changelings, his words very clear and direct, no loopholes for an impish god to find and wiggle through. Roberto glanced at Huitzol and an idea wriggled in his mind, and after a second he whispered something else in the god's ear, like a secret. The paper hands clapped together in delight.

———◆———

It was eighty-seven minutes later that the video came to OPD's Twitter feed. A Mustang peeling into the parking lot of the Eastmont Police Station, doing donuts before skidding to a stop. Cop cars surrounding the Mustang, commanding its occupants to come out with their hands up. The changelings obeyed, and the clip's audio crackled and Huitzol's watching eyes grew wide, and just before the clip ended the music rang out and clear, Roberto's last-minute addition, blasting from the speakers of the stolen car: the chorus of "Fuck tha Police."

Nine years earlier, Roberto had interviewed more than a dozen people who'd lost loved ones to the cops. Photos arranged in shrines in a living room or tucked into a box in a closet or stored in a phone's folder under a dead person's name. He probably could have stopped with three or four people, but their stories kept pulling him in, even as his brain replayed the sounds of the billy club knocking at his ribs. They had shown him folders thick with lawsuit filings, photos of marches, the years stretching on, the thread of their hope growing thinner and thinner until it snapped somewhere inside them, with nothing to do but bleed. He had kept their addresses, their names.

Most of them he'd met through a woman named Amalia Nieto, who hosted meetings in her home and her church. While their coffee grew cold on the table between them, she'd showed Roberto a thick folder full of cases, of bodies, all at the hands of the same man who'd killed her son. This man killed one or two men in each city, waited out the storm of investigations and protests, and then got a job in some new town, sometimes even a new state.

"I can learn how to live with the grief for my own child," she'd told Roberto, surrounded by the puppets and dolls she'd collected since she was a girl. "It's like a ghost beside me, all the time, wearing my son's face. It's awful, but I can learn to live with it. But what about the ghosts that I know are coming?"

Sitting in the same living room nine years later, the sofa was different but everything else was the same. The cop who'd killed Amalia's son now worked in Vallejo, she told him, their coffee cold on the table again. From a shopping bag Roberto pulled out a gift box, and an orchid, fuchsia and white.

"I'm so sorry for what you've been through, Mrs. Nieto. I've been thinking of you a lot recently, and ... well, my daughter Lucy made this little puppet, and I've been thinking it might go better in your collection. He's got quite a back story, I'll tell you. But I think you'll like him. I think you'll put him to really good use."

The Teachers' Association

When Esther Díaz pulled up to Eastmont College Prep at 7:30 on Saturday morning, the parking lot was already full, just like in her nightmares, just like in the one she'd had the night before. Her breath felt like it was stuck in her throat, and she pulled out her phone—definitely a Saturday, no events on the school calendar either. She sighed and got her rolling cart out of the trunk. Every car was neatly parked in the lines between each space, and as she walked to the main door she saw that hers was the only one with bumper stickers: "Education Cuts Never Heal," "Make Gilead Fiction Again."

She felt smaller with every room she passed on her way to room 19, which she would be taking over two months into the school year. Every door had the school's motto: "Work Hard and You Can Go Anywhere." Esther knew what her parents would say to that. For decades they had both worked as union organizers for farmworkers, janitors, security guards. People who worked hard every day of their lives, only to end up in the same place. She felt a stab of loneliness.

She relaxed a little when she saw the teacher's lounge in the main building. She knew she'd find a sad old coffeemaker, a stained microwave, and a row of mugs that would all end up in her classroom by the end of the week until she sheepishly returned them late on a Friday. But as she approached the lounge door she could see the shadow of footsteps underneath and hear a low hum that definitely wasn't the sound of percolating liquid. It was more like a chant, an intonation, and she backed away, uncaffeinated. Maybe one of her new colleagues taught yoga. From under the door came a faint, musky scent she couldn't quite place.

She sighed and dragged the cart into room 19. It was bright and spacious, and the faucets and outlets all worked. Her predecessor had apparently left most of his classroom behind. Pocket charts, an arrangement of cheerful pointers, color-coded baskets for markers and pencils and pens. Esther tried not to add up the cost of what must be most of this man's personal collection as she unpacked her own: the silly magnets for science time, the sentence strips she'd arranged alphabetically in a neat little box that Stephen had built for her. She caressed the purple wood and swallowed back tears. She'd already shed enough in the month since he'd left.

"Ms. Díaz. Is this a bad time?"

The figure in the door made Esther's hand steal to her mouth, where she nibbled at the one cuticle that had bravely begun its regrowth. Jessica Gallegos was the Equity and Improvement Lead, as she introduced herself, thanking Esther profusely for stepping in on such short notice. Jessica was wearing a set of gleaming maroon boots, a yellow jumpsuit (how did she keep dry-erase ink off of that?) and a pristine white sweater. On a Saturday. And, Esther noticed with a sinking heart, she was also gorgeous: impossibly smooth brown skin, hair like a sheath of obsidian down her back.

Esther's own daily look had been dress pants and one of the T-shirts she curated and kept in endless supply. At Sobrante Park Community School, where she'd spent her first two years, it was one of her favorite ways to connect with the kids. They'd pepper her with daily questions about where she'd got the one that read "Nerd Nite '09," or who Pedro was and why they should vote for him. For every The Marías or Tiger Army shirt, she'd mix in her dad's Bob Marley ("Emancipate Yourself from Mental Slavery") or her mom's En Vogue ("Free Your Mind and the Rest Will Follow.") Now she felt herself shrinking inside her Converse and jeans.

"Glad to be here." Not quite true, but it was what you were supposed to say. Esther heard the buzzing of her medication alarm, but there was no way she was taking her Xanax in front of this woman. "And I love that jumpsuit. What a cheerful yellow."

"Thank you." Her eyes flicked over Esther's Bikini Kill shirt. "Ninety-eight percent of our students are free or reduced lunch, and we feel it's an equity issue to dress our best. They deserve to see successful adult role models. And it's only fair: After all, we expect them to wear a uniform."

She'd poured ice water over every one of Esther's T-shirts without even trying.

Two days later was Monday, Esther's official first day, and she stood on the playground watching the painted line reading "19," waiting for it to fill up with a row of eager third-graders. She'd memorized their names from the cheerful little desk tags she'd made. At the first shrill sounds of the playground bell, three hundred children leapt off the equipment or popped up off the benches, strapped on their backpacks, and lined up along the lines, in complete silence. The nervous smile melted right off Esther's face.

Row by row they filed into the multi-purpose room for Monday morning assembly. Three hundred pairs of feet, making only the necessary noise; three hundred mouths, pressed still. She sat at the end of the third-grade row, wondering if she could sneakily snap a picture and send it to Stephen, but thought better of it. Then she looked up. Esther was the only one sitting in the entire room. She caught the gaze of a teacher with dyed-pink hair standing in the next row; a pair of deep brown eyes flashed upwards, the most subtle of cues, and Esther stuffed her phone back in her blazer and stood. The students were beginning to shuffle now, faces all facing Principal Clark, that red hair rising above her lavender pantsuit. Esther wondered what would happen if she just told her students to go ahead and sit. She bit back the urge. *This is a charter school. They don't have to keep you on. Especially if they start asking why you were still job-hunting in October.* Finally the principal's hands gestured toward the seats and Esther heard nothing but a wave of bodies settling and linoleum scraping against metal feet.

The speech was plenty familiar: lots of "set your sights high" and "care for the community," and the metal taste in her mouth began to dissipate. Then the bodies were again rustling, and again she turned and saw she was the only one in her seat. She must have missed a cue to stand, and now the principal's perfectly made-up face was smiling as she led three hundred voices in her call and response.

"Are we smart?"

"Yes, Principal Clark!"

"Are we going to work harder than yesterday?"

"Yes, Principal Clark!"

"Do we make excuses?"

"No, Principal Clark!"

The metal taste flooded back.

⸺◦⸺

At lunch Esther found the pink hair again, belonging to a slim woman in a sleeveless blouse who was rearranging a wall of student artwork, at an angle that let Esther admire her muscle tone. The art wall was cheerful and messy, the first sign of either she'd seen in this place.

"I wanted to thank you for your help back there. That was so embarrassing. Definitely not the impression I wanted to make. I'm Ms. Díaz—I mean Esther."

"Ah, you took over Mr. Ramírez's class. Welcome to the salt mines. I'm Bobbie Ma."

Maybe it was something in Bobbie's tone, the way cynicism seeped through the cracks—the first sign that any of these people had cracks at all, that they weren't just made of pressed rayon and mascara and positivity slogans. Or maybe it was just the sound of it, that self-assured low rumbling that Esther had always loved in a woman. But Esther wanted to tumble into those chiseled arms and cry. She had to settle for an invitation to happy hour at the end of the following week, a small group of the newest teachers. "It's usually safe to sneak away after 5 on Fridays," Bobbie told her just before the bell rang, and if that reassurance was supposed to make Esther feel better, it absolutely did not.

Nor did the offer that came the next day. After lunch, her students were busily coloring in the details on the art project they'd begun on Monday, showing their hopes and dreams for the rest of the year. They'd acted nervous when she'd explained the assignment, and one little girl (Nathaly, all dark hair and round glasses) raised a hand: "Are we getting graded on this?" Esther had smiled and asked Nathaly to help pass out the markers, and now Nathaly was chattering with her friends at the next table about how to spell the word "scientist." MF Doom's instrumental "Lemon Grass" wafted through the speakers and over the room.

"Ms. Díaz. May I have a word?" came a silky voice beckoning Esther to the door.

Jessica. How the hell did this woman never wear anything shorter than four-inch heels and still manage to sneak up on Esther? The class was staring, markers silent and drying in their hands.

"I know this is only your second day, and so of course you haven't had much time to absorb the curriculum we expect everyone to use here, or the approach that makes us so successful. I think I should come and model a lesson for you and your class tomorrow. Principal Clark will take over my class. Will tomorrow at 10:20 work? Immediately after morning recess."

Esther made herself nod and forced the words "thank you" out of her mouth, feeling like a marionette. A five-foot-tall marionette whose black hair was trying to escape from its braid.

—◆—

On Wednesday she sat in her one suit and watched Jessica line up the members of room 19 in neat rows staring at the Smart Board, where Jessica clicked a remote and a multiple-choice question popped up, something about tablespoons of sugar in a cake. At Sobrante Park, Esther had taught her second-graders how to make pancakes. It was a messy, flour-covered project that taught them all the mathematics of measuring and the use of the imperative mood, because at the end of it they'd each written their own recipe and used it to teach their families. She could almost taste the syrup.

"Now, Ms. Díaz's class," Jessica's voice sang out, sweet as two tablespoons of sugar: "I know that many of the third-graders have difficulty with these kinds of test questions. So, for my special visit, I've given us so many of them. Are we ready to tackle this question?"

"Yes, Ms. Gallegos!"

"Are we smart?"

"Yes, Ms. Gallegos!"

Oh, God. Were they supposed to do this every day? And then, as if Jessica had read her mind: "We lead the students in affirmations before difficult lessons. They need every opportunity to hear how smart they are. We feel it's ..."

Let me guess? An equity issue? Esther forced her face into what she hoped was a thoughtful frown, and onto her notebook she doodled a tiny stick figure, screaming into an inky void. At the end of the "lesson" Jessica presented the classroom with a gift: an aromatherapy diffuser that she plugged in right near Esther's desk. A cloying wave of bergamot and something else she couldn't quite place (clementine?) filled the room, a scent Esther had noted walking past other doors. Now it was here.

"May it bring to your class the success it's brought to all of us," Jessica sang out as she said goodbye, and the children took deep breaths, taking it in.

Next Friday couldn't come fast enough.

When Esther finally pushed open the doors of the Laurel Lounge, she was more than ready to take her place with a gaggle of exhausted teachers gossiping over their beers. Instead, there was only Bobbie, perched on a stool and showing off wonderfully smooth legs, and Angie Chávez, who had technically a day's seniority on Bobbie; she'd been hired in a rush after the school had enrolled too many first-graders.

"Aren't the others coming?" Esther hoped her disappointment hadn't leaked into her voice.

Bobbie let out a long sigh. "Rivera and Bittner said they had to get up early. There's a TA meeting in the morning."

"A what?"

"They haven't talked to you yet about the Teachers' Association?" Bobbie asked.

"You mean like the union? I thought charter schools don't usually have them."

Angie's black eyes darted aside at this comment, and she took an urgent pull on her drink before she answered.

"No. Clark started it back when she came here. Thirteen years ago. This meets every Saturday at 7:30."

"Every what the fuck?"

As soon as the words left Esther's mouth, she wanted to pull them back in. Angie hadn't said, *"They* meet every Saturday," and Esther might have just insulted one of her few allies here. But Angie smiled and pulled out her phone, to a photo of two grinning boys, about eight and ten, both with their mother's curly hair and slightly goofy expression. "I only get them on weekends now, so I'm glad nobody's asked me to join yet."

"They can't make you, right?" Esther tried not to let either of her parents creep into her tone just then.

"No"—Bobbie's voice echoed in her lemonade glass as she emptied it—"But, as you said, there's no union here. I'm just glad I've got the new baby excuse. We'll see how long that lasts."

"Wait, you don't mean everyone else is in it?"

Just then the bartender came to ask if they wanted any specials before happy hour closed. They all shook their heads, and Esther chugged her watery margarita and slid a twenty across the bar. For days she'd been looking forward to breathing just a little, to loosening the tightness in her spine she'd been carrying all week. And now she could feel the wire twist inside her, tighter than ever.

She was in her classroom early the next morning, setting up the rest of her library and putting up a batch of student art; by ten she still had hours to go but her head was screaming for more coffee, and so she gathered up the week's worth of mugs and headed for the teachers' lounge. The hallway was chilly and dark, but lit by a faint glow coming from underneath the lounge door. The same cloying smell that filled her room spilled out from under the door; the same low hum from the week before echoed into the hall. But now there was something familiar, the rising and falling voices forming a pattern she could almost make out. She leaned closer to the door, trying to recognize individual voices in the hum.

And then the doorknob began to move. Esther scrambled around the corner and ducked into the supply room just in time, as her colleagues were filing out of the lounge. She watched them through the blinds as they left one by one. Silent. No grateful yammering at their phones, no "Hey, can I ask you about your student Miles?" All of them staring straight ahead, their hands resting perfectly at their sides, all walking at the same pace, and Esther could hear the classroom doors shutting one after the other, like the metronomic beat of a song.

All day she tried only to see the tasks in front of her: the homework to grade, the vocabulary wall to redo. But behind her eyes those eyes were staring, those feet walking all of a pace.

It was dark by the time she could feed her homework packets to the shiny new copier, the last task of the day. She thought of the collapsing machine at Sobrante Park, the art projects she could have made with all the mangled flyers and worksheets spit out by the beast. This thing was humming along, and in that hum she could hear high-heeled boots clacking, the soft scritch of a red pen flying over piles of exams.

In the corner of the supply room was a shelf with spiral-bound yearbooks, a staff group photo at the end of each, and she thumbed through them while the machine stapled and stacked. The room was thick with bergamot and that other scent—she'd decided it was too musky to be clementine—and the fluorescent lights glared down on the photos.

What the hell? This had to be wrong.

Every name, every face, of every teacher, was the same, year after year. The faces getting older, of course, a little more wrinkled, hair a little more gray, but the same. Every once in a long while a face would disappear from one year to the next and be replaced with a new one. That was the other thing. Each new face was shining and bright the first year it appeared. And then the next? Something was gone from their eyes. As if the light inside had been stamped out and replaced with an Edison bulb.

"So you're saying your new school is neat, clean, and well-run, and that the staff has better retention than most private schools—and this is a problem why?" Esther knew she shouldn't have confided in her roommate Zoe, who'd been unemployed for weeks and had never taught anyway. But there'd been no one else home when Esther crawled in at a quarter to eight, face flushed and hands covered in Sharpie ink. It was still too soon to text Stephen. She didn't know Bobbie well enough. Her parents were in some corner of Guatemala with great politics and bad cell phone reception. Esther slumped over the kitchen table.

"Come on; I'll make you some tea. Bergamot?" Zoe reached for the kettle, and stopped when she saw Esther's face.

"Is that ... not good?"

Esther grabbed a box of peanut butter cookies and headed to her room.

Bobbie was out all the next week; she took her kids on a field trip and then came down with the flu. So Esther had no one to tell about the nearly twice-daily visits from Jessica, or the little notes she left ("I wonder if your students are doing enough affirmations? We find that they are so helpful!!" or "I wonder if they should be doing so much unstructured reading?") Sometimes Jessica brought a "gift" that Esther had to smile and accept: refill cartridges for the diffuser, a set of motivational posters, so many and so big that Esther had to take down her favorite Biko quote: "The greatest weapon in the hand of the oppressor is the mind of the oppressed."

On Saturday, Esther got to school at 7:00, so she could get to the supply room before anyone else. She heard the sound of teachers settling into the lounge, but nobody touched the supply room door while she took pictures of every one of the staff photos. Maybe she could show them to Bobbie, maybe to Stephen; hell, maybe a curious reporter would want to write an inspirational piece about this school with its skyrocketing test scores, long wait list, and near-perfect teacher retention. Why was it that nobody had? She tucked her phone in her backpack and went to refill her water bottle in the alcove by the front door.

Then she saw Angie Chávez in the hallway. There was something wrong with her face. Her mouth was stretched, as if she'd been crying, and she was walking towards the teacher's lounge door as if inside it lay her own nightmares. She even turned, looked behind her twice, and started back the way she'd come. Then the door opened. "Ms. Chávez! We were getting worried about you." Angie caught Esther's eyes before Principal Clark ushered her inside, her brown skin blanched and pale. The principal's smile stretched wider when she saw Esther, and her perfectly manicured hand reached out. "Ms. Díaz. Have you come to join us this morning? What good news!"

Esther fled. She was panting by the time she reached her car and started up the engine, and before she even knew where she was going she was pulling up to Sobrante Park Community School. There was a tiny sprinkling of cars in the lot, and she knew one of her former colleagues might walk by as she sat crumpled over the steering wheel, tears dripping onto her blouse. No matter; they all knew what had happened. Every day they all walked by the sapling planted in the yard in memory of Josué, her second-grader who brought his dad's gun to school and pulled it out of his backpack in the cafeteria, so he could show his friends his awesome new toy. It had taken four months of therapy before she could imagine stepping inside a school again, by which time she was desperately ready to take the first opening she found: Eastmont College Prep.

That night she dreamed of a building as large as an airplane hangar, filled with rows of children lined up along unmoving conveyor belts. At the head of each row was a smiling teacher, and every smiling face was the same—except for Angie's, and Bobbie's, and Esther's own. From a podium at the front of the room Principal Clark descended, bearing a jar of salve that she smoothed over Angie's face, and her features melted away until they matched everyone else's. Then Angie's hand descended on a lever and the belt moved, pulling the students towards the corrugated metal door, chains rattling and hinges creaking as it rolled up. Esther tried to warn Bobbie, but all that came out of her mouth were the lyrics to "Redemption Song." Esther couldn't see what waited on the other side of the opening door, but she knew she had to warn the children. As she drew closer she saw that every one of them was Josué, their uniform shirts wet with blood.

⸻⸻◦⸻⸻

Monday morning the recess bell summoned the students, silent as always on their painted lines, and as Angie led her class into the multi-purpose room, Esther found that metal taste flooding back. Angie's hair was straightened and pulled into a tight bun at the back of her neck, and her eyes focused on something Esther couldn't quite see. When Principal Clark gestured for everyone to sit, she beckoned to Angie with a crooked finger, and Angie rose and took the podium, her voice light and sweet.

"Are we smart?"

"Yes, Ms. Chávez!"

As the affirmation repeated, Principal Clark's eyes darted over the room. Esther could have sworn she could see the pattern: Rivera, Bittner, Chávez. That left only Ma. And Díaz, of course.

Recess brought rain that lasted until late in the afternoon, keeping Esther inside with her students all day. She finally found Bobbie just before five, feeding tests into the maw of the copier. Esther shut the door firmly behind her and took a timid step towards her friend. She knew how she would sound as soon as she started to tell it: Angie's face that morning, all the teachers walking in step, the photos, her nightmares, those eyes moving in a pattern over the room.

"Bobbie, doesn't Eastmont seem a little ... different from the other schools you've worked at?"

Bobbie glanced at the door.

"Not here. Listen, I can't make happy hour this week, but are you free Saturday afternoon? I'm going to see if I can invite the union rep from my old school. He's been around a long time and he's pretty sharp."

Esther nodded and just then Jessica walked in, her eyes flickering over them both.

"Ms. Ma. Ms. Díaz. So good to see your dedication. Will you be long at the copier?"

Esther gazed at her hands and counted: five days. Five more days to hold it all in.

On Saturday Esther got to the Laurel Lounge at a few minutes to four and ordered a virgin margarita for Bobbie and a rum and coke for herself. The ice cubes softened and shrunk as the clock swept on to 4:30 and her texts to Bobbie got no reply, and by the time she finally paid her bill at 5:00 they had disappeared entirely, leaving the drink watery and thin.

Esther knew what she'd see on Monday morning when Bobbie arrived. And it was all wrong the second she stepped through her friend's classroom door. Gone were the overstuffed reading chairs, the art wall, even Bobbie's pink hair. And Bobbie's voice was wrong too, that sardonic drawl now a light sing-song that carried across the room.

"Ms. Díaz! I'm so sorry I couldn't make it on Saturday. I got here at 7:30 and I just had so much to do. You know how it goes. Here, would you kindly help me straighten this?" She gestured to the Behavior Chart on the wall, fresh out of the laminator and still warm.

Friday afternoon, Esther sat in Principal Clark's office and delivered the speech she'd honed all week. She'd had plenty of time to practice; she'd slept maybe eight hours in five days. The principal's face was so impassive as Esther spoke that for a second she wondered if she'd actually said any of her speech, or only meant to.

"Ms. Díaz, you understand that the State may revoke your credential if you leave without being released?"

"Can't you see that this just isn't a good fit? Mr. Ramírez must have thought so too."

For a second Principal Clark's eyes flashed what looked like the color of jade. Then she lifted a mug to her perfectly lipsticked mouth, and Esther could see the green liquid inside, smell the tea.

"I will consider releasing you, if you are really unhappy here. But you'll stay until we find a replacement, won't you?"

Esther pictured a room of little faces, the light fading from their eyes each day as a string of substitutes paraded through. Nathaly, who had started begging her mother to go to science camp; César, who stayed in at lunch time so he could read his way through Esther's books.

"Of course."

"I know you've never joined the TA, but maybe you could come this Saturday? It will be such a shock to our little community, losing two teachers in one classroom in a semester. It would be nice if you came to say goodbye."

Those voices humming in unison, those bodies streaming silently from the room. And yet this woman held Esther's teaching career in her hand.

"I'll see if I can cancel my appointment." The appointment she had with a box of cookies and every depressing Depeche Mode song she could find.

The principal's phone buzzed. "I'm so sorry, Ms. Díaz; would you excuse me just a moment?"

She stepped into her adjoining office and Esther had to will her chest not to shudder, the tears to stay safely inside. *Almost there. Almost.*

Just then a text came in: *Hey, it's Bobbie. So sorry again for flaking! Michelle and I have been going through it and the kiddo's kept us up teething and I've been such a zombie. Dying to hear how the salt mines have been treating you. Have they started the helpful notes yet?*

Esther could feel her thoughts doubling, tripling back on themselves. Was the real Bobbie still in there somewhere? Maybe it took more than one meeting, at least for some? What if that chanting was less of an initiation and more of a test? Maybe Mr. Ramírez had failed. And maybe ... maybe Esther was just exhausted and traumatized and raw and this place was bad bootstrap pedagogy and test-prep drills, nothing more?

Back in her classroom, as she loaded up her bag with papers and her grading pens, a text came in from Stephen: *Hey. Is it too soon? How you doing? How's the new job?*

She felt a warmth spread through her chest, a lightness she hadn't felt in so long, and she typed back: *So much to tell you. Job is a story and a half, but I'm actually leaving it soon. You around tmw? I said I would go to this meeting in the morning, but I'm just going to put in an appearance. I should be finished around eight. And then I'll be free.*

The Weight of It

I fucked up. I dropped the jar when I brought it inside the door and the lid popped off and they got away, I heard them escape, I know I did, a horrible dry skittering into the cracks where I couldn't reach and I couldn't see. I tried to remember how heavy (so heavy) the jar was before it fell, tried to tell myself it was the same weight and so they couldn't have gotten away, but I was lying to myself and I can hear them right now. They're in the walls rattling, and they're humming and singing in the air, and they're here when I struggle to breathe, and I know I should never have brought them here and I am sorry. I am so, so, very sorry.

And there's no one I can tell. If I had more friends, if I still had lovers—if I weren't such a miserable bitch, as one of the neighbors sneered after I asked her to stop smoking on the fire escape—then maybe I could have asked someone for help. But then if I weren't such a miserable bitch, maybe I wouldn't have got them at all.

And what would anyone say if I told? I could spin the roulette wheel of lapsed friends, former lovers, a few distant cousins and aunts, and land on one of two kinds of responses. Some would react the way I used to, before I brought that thing here. Those are bedtime tales, I used to say, invented for the stories no one could explain. A man who told of a terrifying month when he couldn't hear any sound, not even his voice inside his own head, and who couldn't make any sound either. He could smash plates at a brick wall, could scream his throat sore, and nobody would hear a thing. Two sisters who ran screaming from their apartment and would never again set foot inside it again, collapsing into shrieks if anyone tried to bring them anything they had left behind. I had always dismissed the explanations as something between a rumor and a paranoid fever dream. A balm against the terror of not knowing.

If I told one of those people, people like who I used to be, they would hear me out carefully, ask me gentle questions about my sleep, remind me how this season is always hard on so many of us, and then text me a few mental health chatbot lines.

And there are the others. The people whose first words would all be some version of, "Wait, why do you have them anyway?" And there would be at least one who would snitch. Would dither, pace the floor, back and forth, and then finally snitch. As well they should.

Why do I have them? The reasons start on the wall I share with the apartment next door, rattling with the indoor football of two bored little brats, the thuds dashing my grandmother's ceramics off the shelves and into shards on the floor. It's in my screaming head from so many nights of shouting, of fighting, of midnight parties on their side of the wall. My azaleas kicked open again and again on the fire escape. But really, it's in Bagel's empty dog bed, dusty and piled heavy with toys, that thuds at me every time I walk past it but that I can't even imagine giving away. It's in a yard gate swinging wide open at the push of a little white paw, car brakes trying desperately to stop. My sobs carrying down the block.

Except that really that's not the why; it's the who, although they're almost exactly the same. Maybe it doesn't matter. Maybe you're right now holding my reasons up next to the jar, fairly vibrating as the things inside seek out their lost mates, and you have no sympathy for me.

How I got them, then. They came by way of a bland little man who reminded me of a damp twig. When he saw me standing next to his gleaming modern house on Heartwood Drive he didn't try to turn around his Tesla and drive away. He just gave one of those fake-friendly smiles, like I wasn't there to serve him a legal notice, half a dozen angry investors rolled up in a single lawsuit. Like I was bringing his tacos, maybe, which is what people of my color usually exist in his life to do.

"Look, ma'am, I know what you're here for. My neighbor's seen you every day this week. But this won't work."

"Sir, I'm a process server, and I just need to confirm that you're—"

"I won't be confirming anything, ma'am. But I'll tell you what. What if I wasn't here?"

"Look, I just need to—"

"I know. You have to do your job. But if I wasn't here and you never saw me, I might have something for you in exchange."

"Sir. I'm going to stop you before you do anything illegal—"

"—What if I gave you something you're not supposed to have?"

He let that settle as long as it needed to, his eyes sweeping over and right through me. Through my rigid face, the frown lines scoring my forehead; down to my faded shirt and the rust overtaking my car. I think he saw a version of himself, a yearning to possess something special, to leap over the rules. He pulled a notepad from a pocket—who still carries those things?—and wrote a few lines before holding it out to me, and we both waited to see what I would do. He smiled once again, the way a snake would look before it stretched its jaws wide open for the kill.

And that's how I ended up in Mosswood Park on a damp afternoon, under a sky that was wet and orange and cold. I stood surrounded by rings of tents, shivering in my damp shoes. That was the kind of weather Bagel always hated. He'd give me the stink-eye when he saw me even reach for his raincoat. The tents were all smeared with the rain, dark shapes inside each one, a faint outline in the gloom, the glow of tiny screens through the canvas. And then I heard a reedy voice call my name, and behind me was a skinny girl with pale skin covered in tattoos and smelling like the air under a bridge. I didn't ask for her name and I didn't get any closer. It was the middle of smoke and virus season and I stayed the fuck away, letting her glance over her shoulder through clumps of stringy hair.

"I thought you might like the Silencers, but they were gone. I have Haunters and I have Eaters." I didn't like the idea of Eaters; I imagined wet teeth gnawing on bone, on wood, on glass window panes, letting the smoke pour in.

"Haunters, then."

She pulled a jar from her messenger bag, a Mason jar made thoroughly opaque from black paint.

"Careful—once you release them, they find the darkness, and you won't see them again."

"'Find the darkness'? Who makes them, Hewlett Lovecraft?" Silence.

"Okay, so how do they … um, what do I do?"

She lowered her voice a notch, and I shuffled closer. "Just put them where you want them to go. And get the hell out."

"They don't kill, right?"

"Would I be giving them to you if they could?" She wasn't wearing a mask and her smile was lopsided, and even at five or seven or however many feet away she was standing I could smell her, sticky and hot, like oil turning rancid. She crossed the space between us and set the jar into my palm, and I could feel it, the weight of it, practically pulling me down. I had no idea why but as I stared at the gloppy black paint I felt even lonelier than I already had. As the girl walked away she patted my arm and underneath the shock, the revulsion, was my flesh warming to hers, after so much starvation. And then she was gone.

So now you know the how, and I've told you the why, but the only question that matters now is the only one I can't answer. *Where.* Because when I dropped the jar I scrambled after them as fast as I could, and I saw nothing at all but I heard them, rolling away like marbles but smaller and hollow, ready to hold whatever you poured into them. Well, the way marbles would sound if you made them of bone.

I sealed up the jar with duct tape and shoved it deep under the kitchen sink and I told myself that, no, no, it wasn't heavier than it had been before I dropped it and no, they hadn't escaped into the walls or through the cracks in the floor. "Liar," I hissed back at myself in the mirror.

It was four days later, maybe five. I was curled up on the loveseat, scrolling through the contacts in my phone for someone, anyone, I could invite over, even if just for an hour or two, my skin almost prickling with the want. And that's when I heard them. Again. They sounded like dozens of tiny bones whistling a song just past my hearing, a song I knew but couldn't remember. I sat up and then it stopped, and there was nothing but silence, hitting like a wave of cold air.

All that night I tried to imagine where they might be, and I kept picturing the slashed movie screen. When I was a kid there was a guy named Pete who had a terrifying acid trip and took a knife to the screen of our only movie theater, opening up a gash the size of my arm. It was going to take weeks for the new screen to come, and they weren't going to lose the revenue for all that time, so we all watched *The Fisher King* and *Cape Fear* with the lights flickering over and through the gap in the screen, and I could imagine anything at all on the other side, ready to pour through.

The next morning I went to make coffee and I heard a sigh, a breath, what could have been nothing more than the settling wood. And I would have ignored it but it came again, and again, and the breaths were coming faster and faster, like my own used to sound when I was gripping a pair of muscled thighs with mine. I heard my coffee mug shatter on the tile. I took everything out of the cabinet and held very still, listening, and there was nothing but quiet. I walked away as softly as I could and just at the doorway I heard it, a sigh with a sob in its chest.

The kitchen grew smaller for me after that. I would hear gasps of joy, pitching higher and higher every time I ran my hands along a cabinet or slid open a drawer. Or maybe invisible hands, scrabbling, as if desperate to find their way out. I brought the coffee maker into the bathroom and let the takeout containers fill up the trash, pulling down the balance of my bank account as the stack piled up.

Then it was the living room. My favorite corner, the over-stuffed office chair, the one I kept when Antonio left. I had it pulled up next to the window so I could catch a glimpse of the palm trees on 9th Avenue when the smoke wasn't too thick. I knocked my water bottle onto the rug and when my hands grazed the floor I felt it, the cold, spreading up from the blue wool, through the fabric of the chair. The cold spread up along my legs and through my chest, and it was actually just as calm as it sounds. It was what happens when panic turns itself inside out. I could feel my heart actually slowing and my limbs getting heavy, as if they were soaked in cold water and slipping underneath the ice. Just so heavy. Somewhere in the distance there was a command knocking its way around, echoing inside bone and trying to be heard. *Get up, get up now,* please *get up.*

I might still be there now if one of the brats hadn't slammed the fire escape door, the sound so loud I nearly bit my own lip.

***

I dragged the chair out to the curb and then two days later the same thing happened again. This time it was my flowered loveseat, the one still stained from when I taught some friends to make pozole, the kitchen warm with steam and the scent of pork and tomato perfuming the air.

I shoved the loveseat down the hallway and tossed it over the fire escape and into the parking lot, the wood splintering against the asphalt. I noticed I was struggling for breath, and now to everything else I had to add my fury at the choking air, at my weeks of isolation with no chance for exercise.

I paced back and forth in the stripped living room, trying to make myself go into the kitchen and take the jar away. But what was I going to do—leave it in Mosswood Park with a note reading, "Danger, don't touch"? Drag it into the police station claiming I'd found it outside? I finally told myself it didn't matter; I had to get it out of the apartment, and I slid down a single shot of Bulleit and went to pick up the jar and it was so cold it nearly blistered my hands.

Then I grabbed a pair of tongs, sturdy things older than I was, and they shattered as soon as they touched the glass. I could hear something moving around inside the jar, another sound like a giggle, and underneath that a soft hiss. I tried to make myself imagine what would happen if I dropped it again and then I just collapsed on the unwashed floor and I couldn't even manage to cry.

And then the darkness came.

———◇———

Ghost was one of the movies they showed so many times, in those weeks before the screen was repaired. There were these scenes where shadows would wail out of the darkness and wrap themselves around the bad guys and drag them off to hell. I couldn't stop thinking about it, those hellshadows dripping through our screen, settling into the drains and puddles of our world while we were distracted by the yuppie ghost. I told my mother, and she said I shouldn't go to scary movies anymore and wrapped me in a hug and I could feel the buttons of her yellow sweater against my cheek. It's the sweater I inherited when she died, the same one I was wearing when the shadow in the corner grew two limbs and a head while I was wiping spilled soda from the living room floor.

I fell in a crumple and I tried to get up and I fell again and it was still there, flickering. Any second now I would hear that horrible wail. I scrambled backwards like a crab, knocked over the hall table trying to pull myself up, and slammed the bedroom door behind me. I cowered in the bedsheets, waiting for a shadow to pour under the door. Where would it go first—the dresser I rescued from the sidewalk, that I had sanded and polished to a shine? The presents from people I've let drift away, reminding me that there was a time I was better, was warmer, wasn't such a miserable bitch?

I stared at the door all night and nothing came, but I never went back to the living room. My world was two rooms now, two rooms and an entryway, and the fire escape, where I could try to coax my azaleas back into bloom.

—◇—

And then the sounds in the walls came back. At first I lay begging silently: Rats, please let it be rats. But I knew better. I knew these sounds, from a memory of camping with Antonio on a moonless night near Point Reyes. They were coyotes, we both knew, but lying there in the tent holding tightly to each other, and now as I huddled in my little bed alone, it sounded the same: like demonic children, laughing in chorus. I snapped on my bedroom light and sat up, but when the light came on the noises choked off. They came back as soon as the dark came back, this time sounding like a giggle, like a cough. Before, I would have called Bagel from his bed on the floor, and he would have burrowed into the space next to me where I could stroke his fur, letting my heart stop its thudding and my breath slow a little longer with each of his.

I ordered lamps I couldn't afford and set them up in my bedroom, letting the light blare into the corners. At night the shine pressed against my skull and peeked around the edges of my shitty sleep mask, turning my sleep shallow and weak and soaked in bad dreams. I started turning in proofreading jobs days late and pockmarked with errors, so of course fewer and fewer came in. I mostly spent the dead hours scrolling through my phone, barely seeing the headlines about the latest mutations or the cat piano videos or the manifestos from a group calling themselves LET IT BURN.

You want to know why I didn't leave. I would have, but of course I couldn't. I could have broken the lease; they wouldn't miss me anyway. But if I did then where would I go? And how could I let someone else move in here now?

I did try going to a hotel, for one night, which was all I could really afford. I got as far as setting my toothbrush out on the sink, checking that the air filters were clean, listening as the quiet filled up the room. And then I heard something, heavy and dense, like a bag of wet sand hitting the closet floor, and then after it what sounded like a series of dry claws skittering away. Dragging the bag behind it, maybe, if they could. If they could follow me to the Comfort Inn and Suites.

That was it, then. I tossed my bag back into the car and drove around as long as I could, watching the sunset in its streaks of blood red. When I pulled into the lot at the back of the building, I could see the side gate gaping open, our cars and the planter boxes exposed. I knew who'd left it that way, of course. The little brats had ignored me so many times when I told them they had to shut the gate after themselves. Had to, always, because Bagel loved to come down there with me while I repotted and watered, and if a skateboard or a scooter rolled by, the dog would forget every bit of my careful training and dash into the street before I could stop him and I would never recover from the loss.

I felt a sob trying to crumple my chest as I closed the gate. Useless things, tears. I wondered if the kids had learned that already. Probably.

I had to take the stairwell steady and slow, and I was stopping to take a breath when I saw them: cracks, spidery and thin, on a wall where no cracks had been. I leaned closer and I could see that they weren't cracks but slashes, and even though it was an inside wall there was white light poking through. I knew, just knew, that if I leaned over and looked through I would see my own self. Maybe younger, joy shining from my face; maybe older and just as alone as I was now but my body stiffer and thicker with pain. I don't know how I got up to my floor. I think I crawled.

When I finally reached my apartment door I rested my hand on the wall to steady myself, and through the cheap thin plaster I could feel something scrabbling from the other side. Not where they were supposed to be, not at all. They were supposed to be in the apartment next to mine, terrifying but harmless, like ghosts rattling chains, sending the shitty parents and their neglected children fleeing with everything they owned shoved onto a truck. This isn't where I wanted them to go, I wanted to tell the reedy girl. It's just where they ended up.

"Hey, hon. How you been?" The voice calling to me was low and a little thin, like coming from farther away than usual. But it was only my neighbor from upstairs, standing a healthy distance away in her flowery housecoat. Bagel had loved her; his little tail would wag so fast when he saw her that I always wondered why it didn't break. I tried to force onto my face what could pass for a smile.

"They talk to you about the heat in your apartment, kiddo?" I shivered, as if on cue.

"Oh, yeah, hon; it's been acting funny for weeks. Warm and sunny outside but like a freezer inside, and then just as quick it goes back to normal again." I tried to take in a breath, but it was as though something had eaten up all the oxygen from the air. *I have Haunters and I have Eaters.*

"Couldn't Beto fix it?" The name scratched my throat as I said it. Beto was the handyman, and he was the one who helped me pick up Bagel's body when the car was done with it. And he was the one who pulled me back when I lunged at my neighbors' door, screaming that they and their little brats were going to pay for what they did to my dog.

"You don't know? Beto's gone. Moved out. Didn't even pack his tools. Wouldn't say why either, but that man looked like he saw death coming for him. Look, I don't go for conspiracy nonsense, but something just doesn't add up. You know those things we're not supposed to talk about? Those things that people say don't exist?"

I have no idea what my face looked like, but I felt like my heart was stepping off a ledge inside my chest, ready to fall.

"You think those things are real?"

"I'm just saying sometimes stuff happens that don't make sense any other way. But it's not like anyone's going to admit it, since officially—you okay, hon?"

I mumbled something that had the words "work" and "thanks" and yanked open the door and locked it and threw the bolt. After a second, the chain. As if what I'd brought home would honor any of those. As if they hadn't already seeped right through the walls, to hurt people who never deserved it.

I ran through the living room, and all around me the air was thick with shadows, dancing and humming, and now I finally knew the song. It was the "Humming Chorus," from *Madame Butterfly*, when she lay bedecked with flowers, waiting for her man. It was pure Orientalist bullshit and yet I'd always loved it anyway, the haunting tune as the ruined woman lay waiting to die. In the kitchen the cabinets were sighing and gasping, as if so close to a release. I wrapped my hands in my dish towels and pulled the jar from where it hid at the back of the sink. It was so heavy I needed both hands to even lift it up and I had to set it down on the counter, my breaths coming fast and my hair swinging into my face.

Three years ago a woman named Tatiana sat on that counter and wrapped her legs around my waist, and I ran my hands through the branching vines of her hair, thick and gleaming a metallic black. In her mouth I tasted Malbec and, later, myself. That was our only date.

"So this is how you work, huh?" I said to the jar. The black paint was scratchy under my fingers, and colder than anything I had ever felt. "Everything that ever brought me joy, haunting me now. That's why you're so heavy." They were feeding off of me, swelling with my loss and my grieving. Maybe with their own fury, the separation for so long from their mates.

"Don't worry. You're going somewhere very soon," I said to the thrumming thing on the counter, to the shadows humming in the other room. "I hope you like bourbon." And I poured four fingers of Bulleit into a Snoopy glass and set it next to the jar.

But first I had to see them, just once, whatever I might see when the black layers were gone. I found an X-Acto knife in the junk drawer, and the jar actually seemed to quiet and settle in as I cut the tape open and began to scrape away the paint. Such a simple thing, an old Mason jar with a rusty lid, calling up an era that never existed, of contented housewives cheerfully canning peaches, sugar thick on the air. The era some people tell themselves we'll get back to if we just stop fighting and let it all burn. Every few minutes I had to stop and rest my hands, twitching and burning with cold. The paint piled up thick on the floor and on the counter and with every layer that fell I strained my eyes, looking and looking for what lay inside, what I never should have brought home.

Nothing. That's what I saw when the last flakes of paint were gone. Just an empty jar with the lid still tight. An empty jar grown so heavy it was pressing spidery cracks on the tile. Empty as my own heart, echoing with the songs I used to sing with my loved ones, our moments when the air was warm and sweet. A hollow, hungry, furious thing.

So now here I am. Wrapped in my mother's sweater, the cheerful yellow a joke, the glass full of bourbon waiting, next to the jar. Any moment now I'm going to pull off the lid, pour whatever I can into the Snoopy glass and make myself drink it all in. Before it gets any worse. Before it hurts anyone else.

Rows of little holes are opening up on the outside wall, letting in tiny pinpricks of light, like a serrated knife against an ivory throat. I picture a slash in a screen opening wide, letting anything come through. The air and its endless strands of viruses, grafting onto each other and weaving over themselves like scarves around our throats. The smoke of the indifferent assholes who don't mind if the whole world burns as long as it burns for them last. The emptiness inside me grown ravenous, come to take over. Maybe it will turn me into a ghost, haunting and rattling inside the walls. I'm already half a ghost anyway.

The dots of light are bleeding into each other, forming a long slash, the dawn ready to pour in. I can feel the walls heaving as if in terror, as if they know something I don't. I am sorry, so sorry, but of course that means nothing now. I toast myself with the glass of Bulleit and open the lid.

Red Brick

Bill was certain he'd locked the door. He always did as soon as he got back in the house, no matter what purpose had drawn him outside. He'd drilled this knowledge into his kids, his wife Lauren, the Mexican woman that Lauren brought in to clean once a week: Lock the door, always, every time. Because these days, you just never know.

But somebody had failed, somebody had shirked their duty, because there was the back door yawning open—no, gaping—and in front of it there was a man. Dark brown skin in a shirt the color of a dirty brick, just sitting at Bill's kitchen table, Thanksgiving turkey leg greasing his chin, the hanging lamp casting shadows on his sweaty face.

Bill's hand went to his waist for the gun that wasn't there, the one that right this second was locked in the safe two rooms away. The stranger didn't move, didn't blink, just stared at Bill's frame blocking the door to the hallway, the door that led to the rest of the house. The eyes were inscrutable, black and glistening like the fat on his hands from the turkey leg, the last one left from yesterday, the one he had promised to save for his wife. Bill felt revulsion cross over his face, and something else like a live wire stabbed at his brain, flashing away too fast to be caught. The man stood up and Bill crossed the distance between them before he could think, reaching for the red shirt that was already gone, that had already slipped out the open door and beyond the reach of the back porch light.

He spent the next hour with his flashlight and his sidearm at his hip, trampling Lauren's poppy beds over and over, checking every single board in the back fence, looking for one that was loose or crumbling or had telltale signs of digging underneath. Everything was as it should be. He wanted to look in the yard next door and even considered waking the neighbors, but his Spanish was little more than a collection of commands, and that was all they seemed to speak. He'd never been able to keep straight who was the father over there; there were about two or three men and women and as many packs of children, sweet little things who squealed in delight on sunny afternoons in the spray from their garden hose.

The next morning while Lauren made breakfast he asked everyone about it in turn, mentioning the gaping door but not the intruder. Amber was, at fifteen, definitely old enough to know better; so was Mason, who at eleven knew he was the deputy man of the house, who even wore a little Deputy badge that Bill pinned on him whenever he had to work late or be out of town for a weekend. Lauren knew how to handle a gun and how to aim at a threat, but Bill realized soberly how she could be overwhelmed; she was the kind of woman who'd be trying to take out the trash while calling Mason's school while pulling out weeds from the yard. "We all make mistakes," he insisted after each of them had denied it in turn. "The important thing is to own up to them and not let them define you." Lauren raised her eyebrow at this last one, and he had to admit to himself, it was a bit much. It was useless anyway; they hadn't left the door unlocked, they were certain, all three of them. Finally he had to let it go and let the kids disappear into their rooms.

Lauren squeezed his shoulders and opened the fridge. "Hey babe, I can't find the last drumstick. Did you clean the fridge or something?" She liked to change the subject by talking about food, but of course she didn't know she was bringing the subject right back. He'd have to fall on the sword if he didn't want to terrify her.

"I'm sorry, I ... you know, midnight munchies and all."

"But you said you were leaving it for me."

The puzzlement and hurt scored her face, but he preferred it to the fear that it was his job to keep from her. She shoved aside boxes and jars until she found the Tupperware she'd packed on Thursday evening, tipsy from the last of the Yellowtail. The container held a single drumstick, swaddled in the layers and layers of plastic wrap she always used. He swallowed hard, rolling the straw place mat in his hands, and then walked away from her face and headed straight for the shower, turning up the water hotter than he ever had.

It happened again that afternoon. Lauren was taking Amber to swim practice and Mason was shooting hoops in the driveway; Bill was waiting for the contractor he'd called out to install a second gun safe, tucked away in the pantry two steps from the back door. The company would come the next day to install cameras and alarms, and he'd have to find some way to justify to Lauren the expense of an installation on Sunday of Thanksgiving weekend. Bill opened the door to wave goodbye to his wife and daughter as they drove off, and the smile bounced right back off of his face as he saw those same cheap sneakers, those tan pants splotched with grease, that red shirt with a dark patch that looked like sweat spreading across the chest. No sign of a weapon in his hands. The man was right next to the path of the van, but Lauren was looking behind her as she always did, trained harder than instinct to look for a child in her rearview, thinking more of the danger she might pose than what was lurking in front of her.

"Mason, get in the house."

The boy looked at his father, startled, blessedly not looking behind him to where the threat loomed. Bill crossed the walkway and pushed his son back inside, putting his body between his boy and danger.

"Dad, what the—"

"Just trust me. Get in your room. Don't come out until I tell you." Bill glanced over his shoulder once, twice; the stranger was standing stock-still at the edge of the driveway, an expression on his face that looked like nothing so much as a smirk. He'd beat this man bloody or blow holes in him, whichever the moment called for. The flash ran through his brain again, just out of reach, an echo of dirty shoes slapping pavement. Bill pushed his son through the open door and the second Mason disappeared down the hallway Bill grabbed the metal bat that stood by the door and spun around. The walkway was empty; the driveway was clear.

Bill made Mason stay in his room while he walked the entire perimeter twice, the bat swapped out for the pistol, not responding to the texts Lauren sent: *Mason said you snapped at him? You were doing so much better, whats wrong?* He didn't like this triangulation, and it was worse when Amber sent him a gif of a burly man breathing deeply on a yoga mat. He wanted a picture of the intruder so he could send it to his family: *this is what I protect you from.* But he'd never do that; it was his job to bear this fear so that they could sleep easy at night. His heart didn't stop lurching until the contractor pulled up.

Then came Amber's swim meet against St. John three days later. The last heat, which she was primed to win. He was sitting on the bleachers at one end of the pool, fighting sleep, lulled and then jerking awake at the elegance of those shapes cutting through the depths, arms slicing through and returning with no wasted motion, the bodies staying effortlessly in their lanes when a simple distraction, a simple slip of attention and focus, would have sent them colliding, with so much at stake. He wondered if their coaches made them practice without the lane markers, where their bodies could learn the practice of keeping their place. He found Amber's flowered cap streaming towards the finish line, flicked his eyes up to the time clock on the wall and there, maybe ten feet away from his daughter, the stranger's feet perched at the edge of the concrete, pool water in a puddle around those cheap shoes.

Bill stood up and his jacket swung at Lauren's face. "What are you doing? Amber's almost—" and the cheers were already interrupting her, Amber climbing out of the blue as the announcer called out her first-place finish and Coach Graham draped a towel around her shoulders and the stranger loomed just behind them both. Bill shoved through the crowd and over to his daughter, fists already forming; people stepped out of his way as soon as they glimpsed his face, casting their eyes behind them to see what could have earned that expression. Bill pulled Amber toward him with a sharp yank on her elbow, ignoring her yelp of pain; he'd apologize later, she'd understand.

The stranger walked directly in front of Coach and waved a brown hand back and forth in front of those green eyes, eyes that didn't react, didn't blink, that never took their gaze from Bill's fists.

Bill let himself turn to see Amber, still rubbing her arm. Lauren was watching from across the pool. Coaches, assistants, Amber's friends, looking up from their phones or each other, questions unspoken on their faces, and not one of them casting a glance at a stranger in a red shirt, smirk widening above that greasy chin, so clearly not belonging, but drawing not a single look.

They were nearly halfway home from St. John before Lauren switched off the Tom Petty and turned to him. "So are we going to talk about what happened back there?" She was driving, which she was usually only too happy to let him do. The back seat was empty; Lauren had got one of Amber's friends to take her home from the meet. East 14th streamed past them in the chill. The sky was threatening rain. He'd have to remember to cover up the metal chairs in the backyard or the next guests would be sitting on a coating of rust.

"Bill?" He hadn't heard that tone in forever. The van idled at a light, and Bill closed his eyes, wondering: If he opened them, would he find the stranger leaning towards the window, grinning and invisible to everyone else?

"Did something happen at work?" Her question seemed to snap his eyes open, and he clamped his hands over them both, rubbing his eyes to cover up the sudden motion.

"Something always happens at work. It's not like I work at a shoe store."

"You know what I mean. Is this about that raid? At the restaurant? I thought you'd gotten over that."

The wire snagged again, live and crackling. A Mexican restaurant, a young man scurrying out the kitchen door against Bill's approaching steps, red shirt stained with sweat.

"I hate it when you call it that. I don't raid anything. I carry out apprehension actions against criminal aliens."

"Oh, so your buddies can call it that, but I can't?"

"What are you talking about?"

"You think I can't hear you when you and Alan and José Luís joke about stocking up on Raid?"

"Those two say that. Not me."

"That's not better. And am I really going to have this conversation with you keeping your hands on your eyes the whole time?"

"Notice you didn't ask what's wrong with them? What if I have an eye infection?"

"Please. If you did, nobody would hear the end of it. You're a big old tough guy until you get sick. So I guess I'm getting the Bill Special. You'll talk about what you want, when you want to?"

"You know, this is really making me feel better here. Thanks."

"Better?" She said it like it was a brand-new word he'd dug out of the mud. He felt the car round the last corner to home, under the wheels the cracking concrete of the driveway he'd been meaning to fix.

"And will you look at me while you talk, for fuck's sake?" She never swore either. He let his hands fall away, one at a time, opening his eyes in little sips, but there was nothing out there. She turned off the car.

"You know I had a hard time making peace with your job. But I told myself someone's got to do it, and that you can set a good example for all those knuckleheads coming up under you. And it was okay. But the agreement was always: You left work at work. Not make us deal with it too. This isn't the first time you've gone back on it. Is it going to be the last?"

Bill's head jerked toward a movement in the darkness, a small furry movement with orange stripes, dashing under the hedges. His relief came out in a laugh that was almost a cough. Lauren snatched her keys from the ignition and slammed the car door, her shape blurring as frost overtook the window glass.

That night he stretched out on the couch, a single broken spring digging into his back, and at some point he must have slept because he saw Amber at the edge of the pool, suited up and ready to go, bathing cap snugly in place, and when she went to jump in he saw that the lane markers were rows of sneakers, cheap Keds interspersed with work boots caked in mud, and tiny shoes gleaming white like baby teeth. He screamed and went to pull her back, and her bathing suit was the color of a dirty brick and soaked in blood.

He lay awake for three hours after that until the darkness began to lift from the sky. His head felt like a rock, cracking in the sun, but he splashed water on his face and drove the Silverado to their favorite donut shop. He snapped on the radio and began singing along almost without thought, tapping the steering wheel as Phil sang about what was coming in the air.

He'd have just enough time to drop them off before work: a maple bar for Amber and the rainbow sprinkles that Mason and Lauren both loved. Mason would forgive the snap and Amber the humiliation in front of her friends and Lauren the breaking of his promise, again, the glue again knitting together the broken pieces. He pulled into the lot and turned off the Silverado.

The stranger was standing next to the passenger door.

The next seconds would replay over and over in Bill's head when he least wanted them to, and when he slid into the driver's seat of a car—any car—or closed his hand around a set of keys, he would over and over again see himself dropping the keys with a shriek that sounded like a teenage girl, fumbling desperately under the seat, grazing a litter of old fries and gum wrappers but nothing metal, even though he'd heard them drop, they had to be there, fingers slipping over pencils and napkins and finally stabbing at the keys, dropping them again before he jammed them into the ignition and peeled off, and he was already streaming along Callan Avenue when he saw it, traced by a brown finger into the frosted window of the passenger side: BOO.

"You all right, man?" Bill's boss leaned into the doorway, taking in the empty packets of Excedrin in the wastebasket, the cardboard cups in a long row between them on the metal desk, each one thicker with sugar and Coffee Mate, the wall clock that barely read 6:54.

"It's nothing. Lauren." His voice cracked at her name. Alan nodded. Nothing new here, his nod said. Bill's stomach rumbled; all morning, anything he'd tried to eat called up those dirty fingers on the window and his own hands, useless and fumbling.

"Hey, man, you ever need counseling, there's always the EAP." He said this the way you'd talk about going to the dentist.

"Yeah, sure. Hey, you remember that raid last month?" In Alan's face Bill could see a whole wall of gears unused to turning.

"That apartment complex? With the woman who wouldn't shut up?"

"No, the restaurant, the one in Fruitvale. The runner."

"They're all runners. What's up?"

"Do we have any pictures of him?" Those dirty sneakers slapping pavement as Bill pulled out his gun. That terrified face, turning back to Bill and his gun, not seeing the alley opening up to East 8th, the cars rushing to beat the light.

"Pictures? Oh, you mean that poor bastard. No, he wasn't even a target. County would have the autopsy photos though. What's left, anyway, after that van fucked him up. You okay, man?"

When Amber was scared, she clung to her mother; Lauren would let herself crumple against Bill, every part of her softening against his bulk. He'd long since told Mason that men had to be made of stronger stuff. What would happen if right now Bill opened his arms wide, if he let his boss feel the shaking that would not stop, if he spilled out the story of the man he had to bear all by himself, the fear he longed to set down for just one second? What would Alan do, this man who would yank off the lights in detention cells when the prisoners whined too hard about the cold?

The laughter cracked open Bill's face. When it finally died he stood up and squeezed past Alan into the hall, ignoring the wheels grinding in his boss' face. He could hear the sound of chairs in the meeting room scraping the floor, voices beginning to fill the room for shift meeting, the room filling with the smell of weak coffee just beginning to burn.

Ten feet down the hall, maybe twenty, the stranger was walking. Nobody was supposed to be anywhere on this floor without authorization, those key cards with the awful pixelated photos on the front. And still here the man was, that brick-red shirt blooming with blood, his pant legs shredded and a tire mark running along his left side. And he was headed for the room full of Bill's coworkers, not a one of them seeming to notice the danger, this man smirking his way through their space. Bill was the only thing between the intruder and them. He slowly unholstered his gun, aiming for the tire mark on the left knee, the barrel dipping wildly under his shaking hands, and behind him Alan's voice rising: "Bill. Bill, what the fuck are you doing?"

He couldn't turn around and take his eyes off the threat. He couldn't advance; that might only provoke. And he couldn't let off a shot, not in this narrow space where it could ricochet back on anyone, including Bill himself. He could hear chairs being pushed back, the voices quieting behind him. But not a single gun being unholstered against the danger, no one shouting out to that smirking face to freeze or get down. Just the silence of a room of men holding their breath. And then Alan's hand closing around the gun, pulling it from Bill's hand, and the sound of a morning's worth of coffee and Excedrin and last night's Laphroaig splattering onto the floor. Bill's eyes shot up wildly, away from the vomit coating his hands (empty things scrabbling) and back down the hall, and the stranger was walking away, no one even trying to follow.

Alan was going to usher Bill into his office now. He would offer a short leave, stress relief, and Bill would have to tell him about this man who couldn't be real, but who had to be real, had to, because otherwise nothing else was.

Bill walked away from his boss, away from all of them. He'd call Alan later. The door buzzed meekly as he pulled it shut.

If he and Lauren had been talking, she might have asked him about the gas. Once Alan put him on leave he began to fill the Silverado's tank every other day instead of twice a week, driving endless miles every day until his usual time to come home, running up the charges on their shared Visa bill. If she noticed, she said nothing. She was never close enough to him to smell the endless cups of sugary coffee on his breath, and she wouldn't see the Red Bull he'd stashed three cases deep in the back seat. She never checked the car, never even drove it without his permission, not after the time he'd shouted at her in the driveway about scraping the paint. The only things she asked about were bland and unimportant: Could he make the meeting with Mason's teacher; would he call his insurance about the kids' orthodontist bill; don't forget about Amber's recital—what do you mean, you have to work?

The stranger didn't come back. Every day Bill just pointed the Silverado down a different street and then drove anywhere he could navigate without thinking, Michael Savage on the radio, volume turned half down but the anger seeping through the speaker anyway. Lauren hated that kind of radio, and normally he played it only to needle her, but something about the spikes and peaks of outrage were soothing, jolting him upright just when the car threatened to veer over the lines. Once he scraped right against the sidewalk where a woman was walking with her two kids. She had the same deep brown skin as the stranger, even had the man's same expression. They always had that same expression: blank, inscrutable, holding something back, some misguided effort at dignity, like Bill was the one in the wrong, like they weren't trespassing in someone else's country.

The day finally came for him to go back to work, and the stranger was still gone. His alarm woke him the same time as always, but his head hurt worse than it ever had, like his brain was hurling itself against the thick walls of his skull, and the lines that had always been there were instead nothing but cracks, from the inside, like an egg. His forehead knocked at the bottle of Laphroaig he'd shoved under the sofa cushions, where Lauren wouldn't see it whenever she walked past him, observing him while he pretended to sleep. How many nights had he slept there? Had they even spoken yesterday?

He looked over to the tall window next to the front door, and through his half-closed eyes he saw it, motion where none had been, breaking the pristine circle of light at the edge of the driveway that kept the darkness at bay.

He was up. He pulled the gun from where he'd been keeping it on top of the TV cabinet, yanking the front door open with a slam against the garage wall, to where the dirty brick shirt blocked his path, flowering with blood that stained the edges of the greasy hair, the heart in the middle like an illegal bulls-eye, and before he even realized he'd pulled the trigger the shots rang out on the street and his cracked voice along with them: "Fuck you, you greaser piece of shit! Leave my family alone!" The street was empty and the lights snapping on all around him looked like eyes, like bloodshot eyes prying open. Opening in a row, the cul-de-sac lighting up, himself at the base of it, white shirt stained with yellow under the arms.

Bill wasn't going to wait for what was coming. He threw himself into the Silverado and peeled off, and before he even hit the lights of the Bay Bridge Alan had called him three times, the last time leaving a voicemail that Bill played and replayed as he headed west. "Bill, Lauren called me, and she's very concerned. She's talked to some neighbors who ... anyway, we need to talk. I'm going to meet you in the garage when you get here. Please call me back." The sun glinted off the surrounding car windows as it rose, and for a terrible few seconds the brightness was all he could see.

He'd ended up in the wrong lane, the one with toll takers instead of FasTrak, and there was no time to shove through the bollards and into the right one. He sighed and slid $10 out of his pocket for the toll. What the hell, he'd let the toll taker keep the change. It was the tiniest gestures of kindness that made the world go round.

He slowed and stuck his hand out the window. The toll taker grinned, brick-red shirt soaked with blood, greasy hands reaching into the space between them.

Someone Else's to Destroy

There's a box in my closet for the things I never touch. Presents from my father, every birthday and Christmas, more extravagant each year as his guilt grew bigger and I grew older without him. His mother's costume jewelry that I've tried to give away but that always ends up back where I keep it. The last thing to go in there was a set of hats for my cousin Imani's twin boys, both Warriors fans though in every other way as different as could be. I'd missed their tenth birthday that year and they missed Christmas, and the hats have been in the box since I finally made myself accept that there wouldn't be any more birthdays for them at all.

How do I describe Imani? "Brilliant" and "confident" are just words. She had asthma and she named the inhaler Vlad. She set the Darth Vader theme as her ringtone. She adopted dying plants and coaxed them into life. She kept her hair natural and curly. She could dance to anything. She grew up split between many worlds and they embraced her and chewed her up in equal measure. Her mother Sandra's family—my family—could never forgive Sandra for daring to have a baby out of wedlock, and worse, with a Black man. They were too polite to close the door when Sandra came to gatherings with her adorable baby and her eternal-fiancé Carson, Imani's dad, but they couldn't manage to remember Carson's name or to resist carrying on whole conversations in Spanish around him. Of course, it meant that little baby Imani learned it too, and even Carson understood more than he let on. His family was different: warm hugs all around and cousins playing tag and their parents happy to play Los Ángeles Azules at family reunions. Even after Sandra finally split from Carson, his family kept on including everyone as if nothing had happened. Same ribs and homemade salsa on the plate.

Our grandmother Maria Inés was a wonderful cook and a truly mean grandma. She was full of snide remarks about why Imani didn't straighten her hair, about how Black men never stuck around to raise their kids. When Imani was fifteen, she'd had enough. She told her grandmother, my grandmother, at Christmas: "Abuela, I love you, but I'm not going to put up with you disrespecting my heritage. I'm not going to put up with you talking like this to my mother or me. If you can't be nice to us, you won't be seeing much of me." She ignored the shocked looks all around the table, my mother nearly dropping the tamales on the floor. Imani kept her word: When she had to show up to family events, she simply refused to speak a single word to our grandmother. It took four months for Abuela to understand that her grandbaby was serious. She gave a half-hearted apology and from then on kept her comments far under her breath. I was twelve then and I thought I would never meet anybody so brave.

Carson was brilliant and confident too, but he was forever starting projects and leaving them half-finished, just like he'd done with Sandra. They'd been engaged for seven years but instead of getting married they split up. Sandra was so different from him that I never understood how they got together to make Imani in the first place. She never made waves, never sought attention, didn't speak much—but when she made up her mind, that was it. She'd let all the family complain about Imani's attitude, but a smile would be creeping at the corner of her mouth.

Imani was used to being the only Black girl in whatever she did. She started a Star Wars club in high school. She learned French. She rode a bike everywhere and was a vegetarian starting at age thirteen. (She told me she'd wanted to be one earlier, but it took her that long to learn to do her own cooking, since that's what Sandra told her: You eat what I cook, and I don't want rabbit food.)

My aunties and uncle—Imani's mother Sandra, my mother Ana, our Tía Marta and Tío Jesús—grew up with linoleum floors and plastic covers on the couches. We lived in what my family called bad neighborhoods and the kids went to Catholic schools. College was a dream that only grandbaby Imani could reach. I went to vet tech school, which doesn't quite count, but Imani went to Harvard because of course she did. And she came right back to Oakland and let everybody praise her up and down.

When she was nineteen, she withdrew from Harvard for a semester and came back home. Nobody really talked about why. She came to a baby shower for our cousin Carolina, Tía Marta's daughter, but she came empty-handed and barely left Tía Marta's easy chair all afternoon. She wanted everyone to watch this movie she'd brought, about a Brazilian slum. She wouldn't stop talking about the kids in slums, the rainforest disappearing, the oil companies "raping the earth while we're sitting here partying."

She didn't look like she was trying to guilt-trip anyone. She was serious. She was crying. I was sixteen and I didn't understand her. Nobody talked to me about things anyway.

She invited me outside; I guess even back then I was the only one who didn't think she was crazy or just wanted to ask her about Harvard all day long. I admired her. I wanted to be like her. But not like this mumbling wraith.

"Mari. How can you stand it?"

"Stand what?"

"My mom's upset because the landlord won't fix the hot water. If she were in most of the world she wouldn't even have water. Or it wouldn't be clean."

"Come on, cuz; this isn't like you."

That was the wrong thing to say.

"Right, because you know so well what it's like to be me. Everyone wants to brag about how smart I am. They're all happy I'm going to go into environmental law. That way they can keep driving their cars and buying their plastic and they don't feel guilty. Do you have any idea what it's like, carrying everybody's hopes on my shoulders? And then those snide little white girls going off to France to go skiing and 'oh, you don't summer on Martha's Vineyard' and they treat the dining hall workers like shit and won't even sign a petition for them to get a raise. I'm not even going back to school. I'm moving to Brazil. I'm joining the Landless Workers' Movement there and I'm never coming back."

She kept talking as if something terrible would happen the second she stopped. Human rights and reparations and she was going to learn Portuguese and there were plants in Brazil that had powers everyone else dismissed as magical, but that was just because people were superstitious about anything they didn't understand, and did I know it was possible to power all the planet's cars on algae?

My mother rescued me just then: "Maricela. I need you to help me wash up."

I'd never been so glad to be asked to wash dishes. Sandra and Imani left soon after, and I avoided Imani the next time I saw her, something I'd never done before. When I saw her at a barbecue that summer she was calmer, more herself. I never asked what had gone wrong with her and she never told me, but she graduated from Harvard and she did go to law school at Columbia, specializing in environmental law just like she said she would.

She dated a lot in her twenties, but none of them stuck around. I'd see her at family gatherings (we had nine cousins), with a different man each year. The men were all brilliant at some-thing, always intellectual: music, science, writing. They were always Black, but Imani had made sure our family knew how to behave. No matter how brilliant, though, none of them seemed to measure up.

When she was thirty-two, she showed up at Tío Jesús' 75th birthday; nobody had seen her in a few months, not since she'd finally bought a tiny little house in Sobrante Park. She got there late, after everyone had sat down, and later I thought this was why she'd done it that way. She was pregnant. She'd got tired of waiting for the right man, or any man at all.

I was shocked but happy for her too. The whole time I knew her, she was the bravest one of all of us. She'd stood up to a Mex-ican grandmother and lived to tell about it. I think even Abuela was proud of her for that, and my mother too, though neither of them would ever say it out loud. I never understood how she could be so brave. I was twenty-nine that year and I still had to endure my mother asking me when I was going to marry my boyfriend Adrian, and Abuela and Tía Marta commenting on my weight, and the one time I showed up without straightening my curly hair they never let me hear the end of it. Pelo malo, they called it. They never said it in front of Imani though. They knew better.

Imani got four baby showers. Four. One from her yoga friends. One from her job. One from her dad's family, where they acted like Imani was the first woman in the world to ever have a baby. And my family's, where Imani was just glowing in a green dress, loving all the attention. That's the thing about her: Even though she acted like she didn't give a shit what you thought, everyone loved her anyway. Maybe because of it.

⸺ ◆ ⸺

She loved to travel. She'd always bring back plants, and I don't know how the hell she got away with it. Oh, she got caught a few times, but just as often she'd show me some crazy African climber plant that took over her whole living room, or something that looked like it would eat you alive if it just grew big enough. Every room in her house had some green growing thing, and you never asked her about them unless you wanted to hear the story about the one she'd rescued from work and that one that came from Brazil and the other one that she was afraid would never bloom and then one day it did and on and on. We all grew up with the stories of our great-grandmother who used to be some kind of curandera back in Jalisco. If you got a headache, Imani would get some kind of stinking oil and rub it all over your head, or make you a cup of tea that would rot your breath. I'd rather have a headache, so I'd smile and tell her I didn't drink tea.

I house-sat for her a lot, and I tried to see how she made her house so warm and inviting so I could copy it for my own tiny apartment. Her place was full of masks and plants and I swear she had like five stuffed pillows for every chair. I'd lie in one of her big puffy chairs, drowning in the pillows, and imagine what it would be like to be this solid, this rooted somewhere.

Most of her plants were beautiful—she had a whole shelf of orchids—but there was one that creeped me out. It was a mess of shiny, waxy roots that I swear made me think of a baby's hand reaching from the grave. A shrunken purple baby's hand. It was the only plant she kept by itself, and I couldn't stand sitting next to it when I drank my coffee. Finally I put a big philodendron in front of it. When I came home at the end of the day the philodendron leaves were curled up, like they'd gone without water for weeks. I moved it back but it never recovered.

I loved playing with her boys. They were the kind of twins who seemed like they were trying to show just how different they could be. Justus was thoughtful, which was a weird thing to say about a toddler. He was quiet, happy to give the limelight over to his brother. As he grew older, he never spoke much, but when he did, it was like he'd been turning his words in his mind over and over before saying them. He reminded me of his grandma Sandra. David was much more like Imani. He was a happy, cheerful kid, charming as hell, constantly getting in one scrape or another and getting out of it through his charm or his brains, or his brother Justus. You'd turn around and David would have taken apart some gadget of his mom's, grinning at you and holding up some little piece, and Justus would be patiently putting the whole thing back together.

—◦—

I got a call one day from the boys' preschool, when they were three. Imani was in court and her mother was stuck home with a migraine, so the school called to ask if I could please pick up my nephews (I didn't correct them.) It was a pretty place: lots of wooden toys and blocks and climbing spaces everywhere, and cozy areas to read stories and outside an enormous sand table and a playground with lots of kids shrieking their little heads off. But the children were white, nearly every one of them, with a few Asian children, and three teachers, all earnest-looking white ladies in their 20s. And two Black boys sitting at a table, guarded by a young white woman who looked both relieved and nervous when she saw me.

"Thank you for coming. I'm afraid Justus threw a chair. David is refusing to leave his brother, and saying he's bad and we should punish him too."

"I'm sorry—did you say *Justus* is the one in trouble?"

Apparently David had got in some kind of fight with another little boy, and Justus didn't like that both David and the little boy both got put in time-out, so he threw a chair.

"That's it?"

She looked deeply uncomfortable.

"We find that these boys have so many problems with aggression, and this is just the latest incident."

Was this lady serious? I was so shocked I took them home with barely another word.

I have to admit, I stuck around Imani's house that afternoon after I brought her kids home, just so I could hear her conversation with the teacher, which she put on speakerphone.

"My child threw a chair. Now, believe me, that will be handled here. But you're saying you can't handle that in your school?"

"We really need to have a zero-tolerance policy on violence. I thought you would understand."

"And why would I be the one in particular to understand?"

Silence.

"I also need to ask: Are you really telling me that you never have little white boys throwing chairs in your room?"

The woman's voice got so high that Imani whispered to me: Someone must have just kicked her in the balls.

"I really don't see a need to bring race into this. I see children; I don't see color."

"Of course you don't."

Imani put the boys in another school.

———◆———

I didn't end up seeing the boys that much for a while. Adrian and I got married a month before my 30th birthday—"thank God," my mother actually said in front of me—but we were in trouble by our first anniversary. I had three miscarriages in two years; two were early, before I even told anybody, but the last was at thirteen weeks. I didn't like what I was learning about my husband, who responded to my grief by telling me to just not feel it.

———◆———

The year the boys were five was the year of Octavius Brown. He was a large, sweet, severely autistic child of 17, and he was shot by Oakland police for not obeying their commands. The fact that Octavius wouldn't hurt a fly didn't matter. He was still dead. We were all at my abuela's house for Easter watching Octavius' face on the screen, his mother collapsing in front of the world. She looked exactly like her spine had turned to paper. Our auntie Marta, setting the table, made the mistake of saying that if Octavius had just followed instructions he'd be alive.

"So the penalty for not complying is death, is your argument?" Imani reverted to lawyer-speak when she was angry.

"No, I'm just saying that—"

"Yes. You're saying that if in ten years, these boys"—she gestured to her sons, and I wished she'd asked them to step out of the room first—"these boys, if they fail to obey an officer's commands, they should get shot?" Imani's voice was quavering in a way she only got when she'd shot right past anger entirely. I don't think anyone else knew it but me. Sandra tried to intervene.

"Mi'ija, this is family time. Not a time to argue with your auntie."

"When she is postulating that the punishment for not obeying commands should be summary execution, for Black boys, for my boys—that's a time that demands argument. I'm sorry you don't agree, especially when we're discussing your grandsons."

Nobody said much at dinnertime. Imani started spending less and less time with our family. I didn't blame her.

———— ✦ ————

The year the boys turned seven, there was another police shooting. Oh, there had been plenty on the news: Texas, Missouri, New York, Florida, North Carolina. We'd seen plenty of Black mothers, and a few brown, shedding their tears on national television. But this one hit closer to home, and it hurt. Raymond King worked in the after-school program at the boys' school. He'd had a hard life, and he'd nearly given up when he heard about a program that trained men of color for support positions in elementary schools. He'd aced the program, earning wonderful recommendations from everyone he worked with, and he was one of the most beloved people at that school.

The news was cruel and incomprehensible and predictable all the same. He'd been pulled over, his three-year-old asleep in the back seat. As soon as he'd stopped the car he'd started filming on his phone. The camera caught the officer leaning into Raymond's window and asking for his ID, and it caught the moment not two seconds later when the cop fired six rounds into Raymond's chest, spattering his wallet with blood. He looked "furtive," the cop said, like he was reaching for a gun. No charges were filed.

I went with Imani on the march to the police station. She'd made a sign: Justus and David, their arms around each other, each with his particular smile. David's was wide and goofy and unmistakable, while Justus looked almost secretive, almost shy. Dark red ink scrawled a single phrase above their little faces: "ARE THEY NEXT?"

———o———

That was the year I finally managed to divorce Adrian, and already my mother was asking me when I was going to get married again. I was the only woman in the family without children, and it's like my mother took it as a personal failure. Imani always went to her father's family for Thanksgiving, and that year I actually said yes when she invited me. I was the only cousin she ever invited to those things. I told my mother I had to work, and she must have known it was a lie but she didn't ask. After dinner, while the women washed the dishes, I finally got up the nerve to ask Imani who that young man was in the picture, the one lit up with a glowing frame in the prime spot on their grandma's sideboard. He was no more than 20 or 22, and his enormous smile reminded me of my little cousin David.

"That's my half-brother. From my dad and his second wife." And she turned back to the dishes as if there was nothing else to say. From outside came the sounds of Imani's boys: David, playing tag with his cousins, and Justus, patiently explaining to one of his "auntie-cousins," as he called them, about the life cycle of the butterfly.

"Have I ever met him?"

"Twice."

"Where is he now?" I knew I shouldn't ask, but the terrible words were already coiled in my throat.

"He was shot. He had on the wrong color shoes."

And now I knew why, with the exception of Warriors gear, of course, Imani never let her boys wear red or blue.

"What was his name?"

"Justus."

The year the boys turned eight, Imani got pulled over one night with them in the back seat of the car. I had to hear about it the way everyone else did, from the grainy video she posted on Twitter. She must have fumbled with the phone, because the video didn't show anything but the passenger window and a chain-link fence. It caught the cop's tone, hesitant, rough, like she was dangerous. It caught him shouting to "stay in your seat, stay the fuck in your seat," but it didn't catch what Imani filled in later: that the one getting out of his seat was David, wanting to defend his mommy. It caught her voice, high and thin and close to breaking, screaming again and again: "Please don't hurt my boys. Please don't hurt my boys."

I dropped by unannounced the day after I saw that, after she didn't answer any of my texts. I'd met someone new and I'd missed lots of events that year, including the boys' eighth birthday party, and I thought she might still be mad at me. I came to her house straight from work, exhausted from a double shift, the street quiet and chilly at just before eight in the morning.

When she answered the door, she barely acknowledged me and instead just started talking, as if we'd been in the middle of a conversation that had been interrupted. She stood on the stoop, and I shivered, waiting for her to invite me in.

"There's no place, is there?"

"No place for ... for what?"

She lifted her chin to the boys, and I actually started: They were watching TV, some kind of terrible kids' show with bad animation. TV in Imani's house was a rare treat, and it was always pre-screened, because she hated for her kids to watch the commercials. They'll get plenty of opportunities to hate themselves, she always said. I'm not paying for them to get any more.

"Do you know how hard I work to keep them believing that they are beautiful, special? That they need to contribute to society because they're part of it? And then all these reminders that they're not really part of it at all."

This was not the Imani I knew. It was as if the ghost of herself she'd been at nineteen had been waiting all this time, waiting for a quiet moment to slip back into her skin.

A sound of something shattering broke our silence. That creepy plant, still sitting by itself in a little table by the window, lay in a pile of twisted roots and cracked pottery on the floor. The boys had begged their mother for a dog, and that year she'd finally given in and got a yappy little white terrier she'd named Clarence Thomas. The dog was growling at the plant, so hard I expected millipedes or tarantulas to be slithering from its roots. He started chewing at them, and before Imani swatted him away he'd bit off half a root and dashed into the backyard, where he hid under the porch, chewing away furiously.

Clarence Thomas actually provided Imani with just what she needed: a crisis to focus on. She swept up the broken ceramics and repotted the plant, which I would have been happy to see get tossed into her compost bin. It was sure to die after that trauma, she told me, but still she gently coaxed its roots back into the rich soil and nested it where it could soak up the morning sun.

It didn't die, though, and Imani went back to work and the boys back to school. The year they turned ten, they grew to be almost as big as Imani herself. And it happened again.

They went to a playdate for one of Justus' little friends from karate; he lived in Glenview. The boys had decided to walk to the corner store and on their way back they passed by a house that their little friend swore was haunted. He dared them to go up to the porch and knock on the door. He didn't know. How would he?

Imani didn't know anything was wrong until she saw the cop car slide past the window, where she was drinking tea. A neighbor had called; she'd seen "two big teenage boys" peering into windows and trying the door. (Apparently the third boy, with his ginger hair and pale skin, was invisible to her.) The cops kept the boys in the back of their car while they waited for a social worker to come and decide if Imani had endangered her boys by letting them walk three blocks to the store.

She wrote all of this in a piece published online, and I was struck by how good Imani was at everything, writing included. "I watched them. Bulletproof glass between me and what I love most in the world. Their bodies were someone else's to control, and maybe, in a few years, to destroy."

You know the saying, "Don't read the comments?" Well, that's true for the way my family talked too. Sandra threw a retirement party for herself, maybe a month after the incident with the paranoid neighbor, and Imani was absent. You'd have thought she wrote an essay about slapping her mother and posted that online, the way my tíos were talking about her. She'd overreacted, my Tía Marta said, as usual. Trying to make everything about race. My Tío Jesús was 86, and everyone acted like age made him wise, instead of senile. He just said: That's always been their problem, those people. If they stopped blaming everyone else for their own failures, they'd be further ahead by now. He said this from his chair in the corner, where everyone had been catering to him all night even though it wasn't even his party. It might have made sense for his age, but he was the only boy in the family and they'd been doing this all his life. And Sandra, the one who'd fallen in love with a Black man, who had a half-Black daughter and two Black grandsons, sat there saying nothing. Of all of them, I was angriest at her.

⸻

Imani always made a big production over the boy's birthdays, but their eleventh came and went with nothing at all. I was busy enough myself; that was the year I moved to Antioch with my boyfriend and was trying to start a family even though I was almost forty and I was pretty sure it was too late. When I try to remember that time I can't even remember when I saw her or the boys. I know I saw them for Thanksgiving weekend, because I agreed to watch Clarence Thomas even though I've never really liked dogs. I went by the house to pick him up, and the boys were sitting at the dining table, heads bent over their comic books.

Justus was painstakingly filling in the color on a comic book figure surrounded by medical equipment and snaking, creeping purple roots.

"Ooh, what's in that beaker?"

"That's an Erlenmeyer flask, Auntie-Cousin Maricela."

"Okay, what's in that Erlenmeyer flask?"

"It's the secret to eternal life. And that's Dr. Severely who's inventing it."

Dr. Severely, clad in a billowing medical coat and enormous glasses, looked like a taller, more sinister version of Imani.

"That's Luke Cage," David told me before I could even ask him about the comic he was reading. "He's Black and he's indestructible. Mama told me it would help me understand."

"Understand what?"

But Imani pulled me into the kitchen just then, and I caught her casting a glance at David and shaking her head, almost imperceptibly, in his direction.

While she was gathering the dog bed and the flea collar for Clarence Thomas, I noticed something. Actually, two things, almost at once. The first was that Justus was wearing a Warriors T-shirt I'd given him for his tenth birthday. The very same shirt:

I recognized the tiny triangle-shaped stain near the collar that had given the shirt a discount when I'd bought it. The bright colors were faded, but it fit him just fine, more than a year and a half after he'd got it. In fact, both of the boys looked the same size as when I'd seen them last, but how could I be sure when I didn't know when I'd seen them last? I stared at them both while they popped edamame pods and nibbled string cheese.

On the kitchen door frame were two rows of pencil lines marking the boys' heights, every six months, from the time they first stood up at all. The dates climbed higher and higher, every six months, until they stopped altogether. The last date was their tenth birthday. As Justus brought the bowl of empty edamame pods into the kitchen, he passed right by the forest of pencil lines, and his head was no taller than the last mark. The one that was already a year and a half old.

I looked up "failure to thrive" the next time I was back at work. None of the possibilities fit: "overconsumption of high-caloric, low-nutrient foods," "insufficient offering of nutritious foods," or, my favorite, "caregiver neglect." This when Imani called the boys' pediatrician by her first name. There were rare diseases, but none of them set in suddenly when a boy turned ten years old. I thought of those lines, climbing up and up until they stopped altogether. The same year the boys had spent three hours in a cop car while Imani watched.

After that, I tried again and again to find reasons to see them. The family skipped Christmas, heading off to some cabin in the woods her boss let them use. She wouldn't respond to my texts. But I finally had an excuse: I'd made it past fourteen weeks of pregnancy, farther than I ever had before, and I hadn't even told my mother yet. Imani was the one I wanted to tell. I showed up at her house on a Saturday morning in January. There was a For Sale sign on the lawn. Imani looked awful. Big circles under her eyes, her clothes loose and baggy. Her locks were frizzy and her beautiful nails were bitten all the way down. She stood in the doorway a long time before letting me in, her body sagging like she'd wanted to keep me out and just given up.

"I didn't know you guys were moving. I thought you loved this house."

"Do you want anything to drink, Mari?"

The boys bounded into the kitchen, wrapping themselves around their mother and reminding her she'd promised to take them on a quick hike if they labeled all their boxes, and could Auntie-Cousin Maricela come too, please? She nodded, slowly, eyes locked on mine.

The day was overcast and chilly, and I felt slowed down by the weight of so many questions I had as I watched the boys scampering along, still no bigger than they'd been on their tenth birthday, almost nineteen months before.

We were walking on a series of switchbacks, and Imani kept warning the boys away from trying to climb a redwood tree whose branches were dangling close to us on the trail. It was tempting, but it was also at least thirty feet down to the ground. The boys were lagging behind us, amusing Clarence Thomas with a filthy, stinking tennis ball that he loved to chew.

Imani stared at the little dog for a long time, saying nothing. I swear she could tell I was gearing up to ask her something, and just then she spoke.

"Do you remember that time he knocked over my plant and was eating the roots?"

She didn't wait for an answer, just kept on talking.

"Well, right after you left that day, he got hit by a car. He slipped right past me to chase some kid on a skateboard. I was really glad then that the boys didn't see it, but now ..."

I waited. There was something about her voice that made me wonder if she was answering my question anyway.

"It was an SUV. A big one, and turns out it was completely full—they were helping somebody move. I saw it. I can't unsee it. So many things I can't unsee."

Clarence Thomas dashed ahead of us on the trail to chase a squirrel, legs working just fine, no hint of a limp.

"The tires went right over him, Mari."

I stopped. The boys' voices behind us had quieted, and we heard nothing but rustling leaves and the wind in the trees.

Imani's voice was very low and very gentle, like it was about to break.

"The tires went right over him. Twice. I saw it. The driver couldn't understand it. But the dog was fine. Not a bruise, not a scratch. He just looked scared and confused. I took him to the vet and they didn't find anything. No internal bleeding, nothing. I remember coming back and staring and staring and staring at that plant. I actually leaned right over it and said, 'I know your secret.'"

"Imani, I don't think—"

That's when we both heard the boys' screams. I swear Imani was off running even before their bodies began tumbling to the ground, down from the tree she'd been warning them not to climb. I saw the ferns shudder as she passed, the redwood branches snapped and dangling where she'd pulled them aside. I made myself hike carefully down, both my hands free to catch myself if I tripped, slow on the switchbacks. My hand clutched my own belly. Over and over again in my mind I saw them falling, their feet still and pointed to the ground, their arms spread wide like an angel's.

When I caught up to Imani she was sprawled on the ground, both boys' bodies in her lap. She looked like a painting I'd studied in high school, whose name I couldn't remember. I called her name and all three heads snapped over to me, and then my feet wouldn't bring me any closer.

All over, right below the branch where they fell, the ground was covered with rocks and roots the size of Amazonian snakes, and a pair of stumps right below the branch, like a pair of open jaws.

The boys were wailing, and she was rocking them both, though she should have left them still on the ground, in case they'd injured their necks. Imani knew that, but who can leave their children crying on the ground and not hold them? The rocks and ground underneath their bodies were clean, no blood, and their arms and legs were curled up around their mother, their arms and legs in shorts and not a scratch, no skin welling up red to form a bruise under their close-cut hair. Not a single swollen patch. The boys looked like they'd just stumbled while picking flowers. Imani was so calm. She was stroking their hair, singing a lullaby I knew myself:

> *One of these mornings*
> *You're going to rise up singing*
> *Spread your wings*
> *And fly straight to the sky*
> *But 'til that mornin'*
> *Ain't nothing gon' harm you*
> *So hush little baby*
> *Don't you cry ...*

The *Pietá,* that was its name, except it wasn't a painting at all but a statue. Mary holding Jesus' dead body in her arms.

Two other hikers had gathered around them, one with a phone in her hand, walking up and down the trail looking for service. Behind Imani, the hiker's voice cut in through the lullaby: "Hello, I need an ambulance at Joaquín Miller Park,

Redwood Trail, about a half mile—" and then Imani's calm demeanor snapped: "No, please, I'll take them." I could hear her trying to keep down the panic in her voice.

"Ma'am, these boys need to get to a doctor. They could have internal bleeding, they could have a concussion. I know you're freaked out, you're not thinking straight."

"I said I'm taking them."

You could tell the woman wanted to argue further, but what could she do—call the cops instead of an ambulance? We all waited to see if that's what she would do. Instead, she shoved the phone into her pocket as she watched the boys stand up, quiet now, even the dog waiting to see. The dog who should have been dead, if you could believe Imani's story.

The car ride back home was completely silent. What I'd seen was hanging from the windows, it was billowing out into the air, it was streaming from the exhaust pipe. It jogged alongside us at every red light. As we passed right by Highland Hospital, Imani looked at me, and her sons, and kept right on driving. The boys were playing with some puzzle thing, absorbed as anything.

"How about some ice cream when we get home, guys?"

"Rocky Road, Mama?"

"Strawberry?"

They should have been entering the age where they started to pull away from their mother, and definitely wouldn't be calling her "Mama." Her face softened when she heard that: blurred, then hardened again, then blurred as she turned off the freeway to home.

"Auntie-cousin Maricela, what kind of ice cream do you like?"

I hated ice cream. But the car was slowing down and pulling toward home, and I was putting together everything I knew from the boxes piled up and those lines that went nowhere and the boys walking away without a scratch from a fall that should have broken them into half a dozen pieces. And Dr. Severely and Luke Cage. And Raymond King and Octavius Brown. And so I smiled and said, "Strawberry and Rocky Road and whatever your mother's having. All in a big bowl."

Justus rushed into the house when we arrived, followed closely by David, running for the bathroom. Imani stood at the front door for a long time, and her body looked like it was fighting to bar me from the door but also let me in so she could throw herself on the sofa and sleep for a week. All of them together. My question tumbled out of me before I got inside the door.

"Imani, are the boys ... okay?"

"They're going to be okay forever. I made sure of that."

"What did you do?"

"You don't want to know."

And that was that. She held my gaze with hers, those eyes that shimmered with tears and dared me to challenge her, all in the same stare. She headed for the kitchen to serve the ice cream.

"Are they ever going to get older?"

"No. They'll never get shot for reaching for their wallet either. Or wearing the wrong color shoes."

"They'll never fall in love. They'll never give you any grandchildren."

"What do I want with grandchildren I can't protect?"

"Who's going to take care of them when you're gone?"

"I'll figure it out."

"How could you do this?"

"Think about the child you're growing. Might be the only child you'll ever have. Wouldn't you?"

This part of the conversation didn't even happen at all. Well, it did, but in my head. Like if I just didn't say it out loud it wouldn't be real. The little marks on the wall would climb higher and higher and someday the wall would get new lines and the names of grandbabies that Justus or David would lay in Imani's arms.

———

I came back the next week and they were gone. Emails bounced back, phone number disconnected, all social media deleted. I didn't know any of her father's family, not really, and anyway what would I say?

She sent her mother a postcard that year at Christmas. No message, no pictures of course: just their names. The boys' signatures look just like a ten-year-old's should. No return address.

I've never seen them since, not anywhere. Never heard from any of them. None of the family has. Sandra's memory has been fading, just a little; whenever she talked about the boys, they were always still ten years old. I like to think this was how her mind protected itself against what it knew. Maybe she never knew at all. I've wondered so often why I'm the one who knows, why Imani let me come with them that day, why she let me see anything of what she'd done. All I've come up with is this: I was the only one who might understand.

That day we went to Joaquin Miller was the last time I saw any of them. After awkward conversation over ice cream, they all three walked me to the door, polite as always. Imani had a hand around each boy's shoulders, and their heads reached almost to their mother's, the highest they would ever get to be.

The Unburied

Later, Dave would try and try to remember the name of the guy on the crew, the one who had stood in the trailer's doorway as the machines fell into silence behind him, holding something wrapped in blue cloth. The crew guy looked kind of young and vaguely familiar in the way that half the workers on the site reminded Dave of somebody else, or each other. Dave could hear the stream of voices outside, everyone louder than usual as they headed home, as if they could already taste the beer, whatever it was they drank, cold and welcome on a day like today. Everyone except this one, whose name Dave hadn't caught, or had caught and dropped again. And who was asking something now, something about the site superintendent, who for once wasn't here.

"Enrique left. Probably up at that Irish bar in Jack London." *Which is where you should be*, Dave hoped his tone hinted at. When the kid didn't move, Dave sighed and stood up from his desk.

"Is there something I can help you with?" Dave leaned next to the photo where he stood, flanked by Marty and Andrew, the

M and the A of DMA Development, all three of them grinning and breaking the ground.

"Yes, sir. I found this out on the site, and I thought someone should see it." The guy coughed into his fist. "It looks old." That was a great word to hear at a $400-million construction site, the earth already opened, smoothed, prepared for the concrete that would be coming tomorrow. Dave didn't want that thing coming any closer. But here it was now, the kid setting it down on the desk, real careful, unwrapping the blue handkerchief.

Eleven years, Dave thought as they both stared down at the cloth. That's what had already been invested in the planning and designing and approvals and geotechnical surveys and eighteen months of scraping and digging and drilling this earth. Getting it ready for the moment that the skeleton of Brooklyn Landing would finally begin to rise. Dave turned back to the kid, dark eyes in a narrow brown face.

"I appreciate your diligence, but I don't think this looks Ohlone." Dave was amazed at how quickly this rolled off of his tongue.

"I heard this was one of those shell mound sites. Like a burial ground."

Now it was Dave's turn for a coughing fit. "No, that's a rumor. We had to get all that evaluated before we got any of our approvals. This place is in the clear." But the dusty figure on the desk stared up at them both, shoving a crack into Dave's certainty. He felt a prickle along his spine as he stared back at this thing that might have lain undisturbed for hundreds of years.

His eyes lit now on the phone in the kid's pocket.

"You didn't get any good pictures? Of where you found it, I mean?"

"No, sir; my phone kind of died." This was looking better and better.

"Maybe someone else did?"

"I didn't show anybody else." And with that the movie clicked off, the one playing inside Dave's head: of the operation screeching to a halt, the weeks of studies and consultations, the crew guys standing around collecting pay while doing nothing, the breathless articles and the awful headlines. And for what? This thing that was probably nothing at all.

"I'll make sure it gets looked at. Just to be thorough." Dave stood now and opened the door and the kid took the hint, glancing back at the desk once more before he walked out.

The headlights of his Tesla were stabbing into the dark as Dave pulled up to the far northern edge of the site, next to a graffiti-covered No Parking sign. There wasn't anyone who could have seen him as he clambered down the rocks and tossed the bundle into the Oakland Estuary. He heard it splash and then he slid behind the wheel and drove into the hills, to his house on Arrowhead Drive.

That night in his bed he heard drumming.

•

When it began he could drown it out, sort of: He could slip on headphones and turn up the white noise as loud as he dared, and let Liz snore in oblivion beside him, her breath soft as sweet peppermint. But then a night or two later he would have to turn up the roar's volume again. When he could force it no higher, he called Dr. Chan, mumbling vaguely about stress and insomnia.

First came Restoril, and with it came horrible dreams: of floating through marshy land littered with bones, of walking over black earth that opened wide and pulled him in. It was the same with the Sonata and Belsomra and Zolpidem. He would pour down endless cups of black coffee while he walked through the site, his hands sped-up and shaking and his thoughts muddy and weak. The higher the building's frame grew, the stronger his nightmares got. He backed out of going along on his daughter's college visits with Liz, backed out of their anniversary weekend in Baja. Liz began suggesting, then asking, then begging him to see another doctor, see anyone else.

He knew what would happen the moment he did; the disbelief that would cloud the doctor's face, the labels that would stick like glue. So he had to keep putting her off, her impatience stretching thinner and more brittle each time. As the weeks went on they both knew that if Hannah weren't there it would have already snapped.

"Are you going to do anything to fix this?" she asked, the night he nearly fell asleep driving them home.

"Yes," he muttered, slamming the guest room door.

But there was nothing to do, not really. When he drove past Crown Liquors one evening, it felt like the only place left to go, never mind the eight-year sobriety chip rattling from his keys. And, sure enough, he slept like an angel that night, the Tanqueray drifting through his blood.

———

Then came that April morning, cloudy and damp. Dave was walking across the southwest corner of the site, watching the cranes swallow up stacks of I-beams and spit them into rows of red steel. He could see one of the crew guys approaching, and by the time he saw the tattoo on the guy's wrist it was too late, the guy was too close, and Dave braced himself for the question he knew he deserved.

"So was everything okay, Mr. Hooper? With that thing I found?"

Dave made his voice as close to cheerful as he could.

"Absolutely. Nothing to worry about." The kid looked old enough to be skeptical, but not old enough to know what to do. Dave gestured at the beams all around them, to the spine of the building, four stories already formed, its metal ribs looming over them both. "See? Proof is right here." And he knocked at the beam with his fist.

Dave would always remember the order of what happened next. First was a sound like the earth itself, like the earth howling in a cheated scream. Only then did the ribcage of the building start to shake, a shuddering that traveled along to its spine. Nothing else shook: not the trees nearby, not the cars in the lot. Only the building itself, as if all of it had always been weak, the bones and the ground underneath. And only then was the howl drowned out in the roar of the spine collapsing into itself, pulling its ribcage down with it onto the ground, the metal beams painted in rusty red.

⟡

"Dave, how you feeling? Do you need a minute?" Dave snapped his eyes open; in front of him his computer screen was filled with rectangles, the largest one now lit up in green. A voice—Andrew's—crackled out from the speakers. There were other boxes, holding faces he knew: three risk and compliance officers for Whitman Capital Group, the grantors of Brooklyn Landing's construction loan. The rectangles were all the same size, in the same place, as the ones that had filled Dave's screen all day long in the three days since the spine had collapsed. Different faces, different names, but delivering bad news, every one of them. These would only do more of the same.

"Dave? I was just asking about some of the on-the-ground reports? After the incident?" Andrew's Zoom background was from his last trip to Hawaii, the ocean framing him in a halo of blue.

"Of course. The ground. I was the only one who heard it, you know. It's my curse to bear. Have you ever heard the earth howl?" There were eight people on his screen all together, and now all of them looked away, or blinked as if they had dust in their eyes.

"Um, Dave, I remember you telling me some really reassuring news. By the grace of God, only a few injuries. In fact, didn't you say all of our guys made it home?"

"It's okay, man. You think you can hear the gin in my voice, but don't worry, everyone. I made myself skip it last night. I only take enough to sleep anyway. Not like it works anymore. I think I slept maybe a week ago? I dunno; ask the drummers." Andrew's eyes were darting all over the screen, as if he'd forgotten he wasn't the host and couldn't mute anyone. The compliance rectangles were going dark now, and a few of them disappeared.

"Dave, I think we're going to sign off. Let's pick this back up at another time."

Dave wasn't sure which of them had spoken, but the faces were all blinking away, one by one, and now the only face on the screen was his own.

There must have been a moment, he thought, a time when he could have told Liz, and now he'd missed it and it was too late. How could he confess that he'd ignored the lessons from all those horror movies she loved? Or that as the investigators tried and tried to understand the frame's inexplicable collapse, he knew the true reason why—and that it was all because of a figure wrapped in blue cloth? Instead he slept in the guest room, avoiding Hannah and Liz, grateful every night he heard only drumming, nothing worse. He was in the guest bed on that weekend in May when he woke up and slung his feet over the bed and the carpeted floor was gone.

Under his feet was something like straw, or maybe reeds, woven impossibly tight and strong. He could feel cold air underneath, as if the house's floor and very foundation had rotted away. He didn't dare turn on the light, didn't dare move. If he took another step, this would all become real, the worse thing he had known was coming.

Through the doorway he could see the dining room, lit by the waning moon. He could see Hannah's soccer bag and her cleats, her lucky ones, tossed on a dining room chair. And the chairs, the new ones, the ones he and Liz had picked out months ago. And a giggle cracked open Dave's throat.

"Haha, not so fast!" He was shouting, but he didn't care. A door thudded open upstairs and he ignored it. This was a dream, and he'd noticed it just in time: In real life the new chairs hadn't yet been delivered, and Hannah wasn't back from her soccer trip.

"You can't fool me!" If he could scream loud enough, he might just wake himself up, and then feel everything under his feet as it should be, the carpet soft over solid wood.

"Dave?" And the lights snapped on in the kitchen and there was Liz, slack jawed and staring, Hannah a few steps behind.

"But you can't be here," he pointed at Hannah. "You're still at your tournament."

"We got back last night, Dad." Hannah took a step toward him and Liz actually stuck her arm out and pulled their daughter back, away from him.

"But the new chairs weren't here. They weren't here yet." But that was wrong too, said the lines across Liz's forehead. "They got here a week ago, Dave." And she took Hannah's hand and he could hear feet padding upstairs and a few minutes later car doors snapping open, and what must be overnight bags tossed into a trunk.

Her text came in a few hours later. She'd made an appointment for them both with a therapist, the same one they'd seen eight years before. He tried to imagine himself stepping through the doors. What would the office become, if the very ground under his feet could change underneath him? Would the doors open to long tunnels, the walls made of dried bones, whistling in the chilly wind?

He didn't go to the appointment. He didn't respond to Liz's calls, her messages. The takeout containers piled up on his counter and he watched *Fight Club*, watched *Die Hard* until he could quote Alan Rickman's lines better than Alan himself. A week after the appointment a knock on the door came while Hans fell and fell, and he knew before he'd even signed for the envelope just what it would hold. It was from the same firm that had handled his prenup, and he buried it in the compost pail. He'd done the same with the letter from Andrew and Marty, the one severing him from DMA Development with a bank transfer and a flourish of ink. He knew he was just kicking the can down the road, but whoever had come up with that phrase must not have known just how satisfying it could feel, the adrenaline thrill of that kick.

The AA meeting was held in the library's community room, and he stared at the faded khakis, the worn-down shoes. Salt of the earth, his father would have called them, and he'd always rolled his eyes, but maybe it was true. Maybe these people were just what he needed. To remind him that no matter where you were on the totem pole of life, you could still be brought down by the darkness in your own soul.

Dave gulped from his bottle of Fiji water, swaying slightly as he rose to speak.

"I've been sober eight years. Until recently. I told myself I didn't need meetings, anything. I was so wrong. Because I came right back to the gin a month or two ago when everything I worked for so hard started falling apart. And it's all my—"

Dave stopped. There again came the drumming, finding him even here. But this time as he stared at the humble faces around him he could hear the rhythm he'd been ignoring before. *You know what you did. You. Know. What. You. Did.* And it would never end, would it? Not until he faced it, until he owned up.

He pushed through the rows of chairs, practically ran to the parking lot. And, as he started up the engine, he could hear the drumming stop.

His headlamp blared into the darkness as he clambered down the rocks just beyond the graffiti-covered No Parking sign. Its light must be visible at least a mile away, but unlike last time he was ready to be seen. Hell, even caught.

The new thigh-high wader boots made his legs slow and clumsy, and he kept slipping off the sharp rocks. He'd forgotten to buy gloves and his bare hands kept scrabbling at glass bottles, plastic bags, drink lids, cardboard cups: everything but a tiny object that might still be wrapped in blue cloth.

He could hear the wind whipping around his ears. He stumbled again, fell again, and his scraped hands bled over the rocks. He was sure to get an infection, something coursing through his bloodstream, trying to destroy him from within. But this blood might be the sacrifice he was supposed to make, and he was sure of it as his raw hands fumbled again in the dark water, because now something was brushing against them, something wrapped in a handkerchief, smelling of duckweed and mud.

He shoved through the doors of the Native American Cultural Center just after ten the next morning. He knew what the receptionist must be seeing: a wild-eyed white man with a stubbly beard and hands covered in cuts, asking to speak with Adam

Ortíz. "Adam was my roommate at Stanford. He took me to a pow-wow once."

Adam was grayer and rounder than he'd been back at school, and he leaned over the conference room table as he listened, the furrow between his eyes thickening.

"Dave, my expertise is in oral histories and storytelling. And I'm Tewa. I grew up in New Mexico."

Something tightened inside Dave's chest. "I'm sorry; college was forever ago. Are you still friends with that museum guy? Maybe we could show this to him." Adam's eyebrows shot up at the word "we." But he took a deep breath and left the room, coming back ten or so minutes later with a laptop and a fuzzy face on a Zoom call: a friend of Adam's from grad school, now a curator at the Oakland Museum. Two of Adam's co-workers stopped in the hallway, peering through the glass wall.

For the third time that morning Dave explained everything, but now the friend sighed and asked to see what Dave had. He could feel a swell of adrenaline, the thrill of consequences finally to come. He peeled back the cloth and held the artifact up to the screen.

And then the computer rattled with laughter. It spread to Adam, to the two coworkers, the receptionist who came from behind her desk. It was like a joke everyone was in on but Dave. The curator plucked something off of his shelf, littered with objects of shell and obsidian.

"Does this look familiar?" And indeed, the screen filled with a twin of the little clay figure in front of them, this one mounted to a cheap plastic base. Dave could feel his limbs turning cold.

"That's not a native artifact at all, my friend. It's a piece of memorabilia from the Lone Ranger Museum. You can buy one for $12.99."

Hot and Cold

Ellie cursed and slammed her battered '09 Kia Soul into the parking lot of the closed Treasure Island Market and Deli. *This is what you get for never checking the oil,* the critic inside her growled as she watched the heat indicator fly up to a terrifying angle, smoke leaking from the edges of the hood. The November night was so cold she could see her breath in the air. "Couldn't wait until payday, could you?" she tossed over her shoulder as she slammed the door and let the car mutter itself into silence. Her phone had no service, still; there'd been no service on the bridge either. Above her on the bridge the traffic thickened, the same traffic that she'd been stuck in, overheating her car. The same traffic that had made her late to the warehouse party DJ gig, that she'd been just desperate enough to accept. A chorus of horns began to blare. It was after one in the morning, way too late for the traffic to be this choked up. Must've been an accident or something.

She watched the brake lights glowing in the fog, and she imagined every one of the drivers holding blessedly operating phones, their calls and their texts bleeping and blooping into the air, a cacophony of signals and humming and buzzing, an invisible net in the sky. She wanted to pick up any one of the beer cans littering the lot and toss it in mute fury at their heads.

Still no reception, which meant no AAA, no Uber, no calls to the one or two people who were still in her life and who she could disturb in their late-night beds. She walked to the edge of the lot. Still nothing, even when she tried 911. This wasn't exactly an emergency, if you didn't count being broke and forty-six and behind the wheel of a rattling car wheezing and begging to die, fog swirling in and around like the breath of a woodland creature with terrible claws. The phone made a half-choked ring before informing her that her emergency call had failed. Over and over again.

She tossed the useless thing onto the seat and yanked open the trunk. The can of coolant was buried underneath half-empty boxes and bags of trash, but she could tell what was wrong the instant she picked it up. She'd used all of it up the last time, she remembered, and then tossed the empty can back into the trunk until she could recycle it, so she wouldn't be dumping chemical residues into the groundwater. *Nice work*, the critic smirked.

She turned to look back where she'd come from, the Oakland skyline lit up with the distant flash of a siren. At the far edge of the lot, against a chain-link fence, was a clump of cars with the windows shrouded in what might have been tarps, blankets smeared with dirt, camouflaging the unlucky humans inside. One of them had popped open their door and was making her way over to Ellie. She was a small pale woman in a forest-green down coat that looked wonderfully warm. Her deep brown eyes took in the overstuffed crate in the back seat, the scrapes against the Soul's passenger side, Ellie's jacket with the tear along the waist.

"New here?" The tone was soothing and free of all judgment.

"No, I ..." Ellie let herself trail off. The paths that could lead her away from this lot were all vanishing fast. Her eyes lit on the glowing phone at the visitor's side, but the woman shook her head.

"Sorry, hon; you'd be welcome to use this if it had any reception right now. It's useless; so's everyone else's." Her chin pointed to the other two cars next to hers, faint hints of movement behind the shrouds. "Even my partner's phone is out, and she always has service. You're welcome to try mine for yourself, but please don't throw it or anything."

"Why do you say that?" Ellie's journalism training sneaked in at the oddest moments, like now, asking open-ended questions, letting people talk.

"I saw you pacing and stabbing at your phone," the woman said. "Looking like you wanted to throw it in the bay." She looked to be in her seventies, but she was sleeping in a parking lot, cold water and dark concrete all around her. *That'll be you some day when you're too old to work,* the critic stabbed from inside.

"Yeah, I'm late for a gig, and my car's ..." Ellie looked over her left shoulder at the bridge. Even once the radiator cooled, even if she had gallons of water to pour down its throat, it would overheat again in no time in that unmoving snarl. "My car's had it. I guess I should just call an Uber or something." She could picture the driver, watching as she unloaded crates of records and a dusty turntable into his car, the car he probably slept in overnight between rides. Which of them would pity the other more?

She tried the phone that the woman handed her, even as she knew exactly what she'd get. Nothing. Up on the bridge the engines were now beginning to turn off. Could she hike up there on that curving dark road, find a call box? Maybe walk further into the island, to the cheap housing projects at the other end of the road? And do what—just start knocking on doors, asking to use someone's phone? And if she did leave her car to do either, would she come back to find her windows smashed and her records and turntable gone, the falling away of another splinter of her livelihood? Ellie knelt to the ground, feeling suddenly every bit of the exhaustion that she'd been fighting for days. Fighting for a long time, if she really let herself think about it. Picking herself up after a crisis took more energy each time, and now it looked like she'd have to do it again. *Good luck getting more DJ gigs now,* said the critic. *Another bridge burned. You're good at burning bridges. Remember when you were bartending at the Red Crow and you threw a hot toddy in the owner's face, to teach him to keep his hands to himself? No more bartending jobs for you after that.*

Then she saw that the small woman had gone to her car and come back. The skin of her hands was pale pink, like the inside of a seashell, and they were holding out something large and bright red.

"I thought you could use this." It was a sleeping bag, encased in a trash bag and spotlessly clean; Ellie could smell the whiff of fabric softener through the plastic, and her frigid hands reached for it almost in spite of herself.

"Thank you. I'm Ellie. What's funny is my last name is Jardines, but I kill every plant I touch."

"Terry. Like the cloth from the towels." She grinned and something inside Ellie loosened, just a bit.

She couldn't wrap herself up too tightly in that thing or she'd never be able to stay awake. But she settled herself onto the seat and her shoes onto the floor, and Terry reached through the window to help her pull up the zipper. Before the zipper made its way up, Ellie slid the Club from the back seat and pulled it into the bag. Terry laughed.

"Don't worry about that. Nobody messes with you here. Except sometimes drunk assholes come out here after the bars close and harass us." *Us.* Jesus. She patted Ellie's hand and shuffled back to her car.

Up on the bridge the chorus of horns had quieted, as if their owners had finally resigned themselves to the wait. She tried to imagine the people up there, stuck on the bridge in the dark morning hours. Security guards, restaurant workers, Uber drivers. Maybe a DJ or two, like her? She could see a few doors popping open, even in the chill. Her body began to relax inside the warm, dry cocoon, exhaustion and fear battling inside her chest. Through the fog of the window she could see the lights of the Port of Oakland. Forty years her father had been a longshoreman there. His midnight-blue Chevy always so bright and warm when it came by to pick her up from school every day, the speakers bumping out the War and Malo and Santana he loved. Sometimes he'd grin and pop in Black Sabbath or Guns N' Roses, and together they'd shriek out the chorus, their voices rising high and her little hands thumping at the soft leather seats.

There was something thumping at the car. There was something shrieking, but it wasn't Ozzy from the speakers. There was no Chevy, only her battered Soul with the tear in the passenger seat, and she was wrapped in a sleeping bag and she couldn't feel her hands and a blurry green shape was pounding at the window and it had a woman's voice, speaking so low she could barely hear it, something that sounded like, "Let me in!" Ellie yanked at the sleeping bag's zipper, but her fingers were stiff and useless and so she clawed the bag away from her like dead skin. She recognized the forest-green color, and that voice, now stripped of anything but fear. *Don't be stupid; don't open that door,* the critic hissed, and Ellie ignored this and unlocked the doors and Terry clambered onto the passenger seat, her face blanched white and her mouth gibbering and struggling to form words.

"Is it really dead?"

"Is what dead? What happened?"

"Your car. It really won't start? Please try. They're going to get us. I saw it."

Ellie couldn't put those words into any kind of sense. But it didn't matter in light of that face. Her shaking fingers dropped the keys, found them, dropped them again, and when she finally turned them in the ignition they both heard the whirring of the starter motor she'd been trying to replace, the engine turning and turning and not catching and not catching. Her phone responded to nothing, like the engine, like her brain, that could make no sense of the shivering, sobbing woman next to her or the words coming out of her mouth.

"They got her. Why did they look like that? Where did they come from?"

And Terry smeared away the frost from the windows and pointed a shaking finger towards the bridge. What Ellie saw there couldn't have been a dream, not with her teeth chattering so hard she nearly bit her lip, but it also couldn't be real.

The bridge was littered with bodies. Draped on the hoods of the utterly still throng of cars, or half-dangling over the sides of the bridge. No blood, no marks, none that she could see from here. Coated in a thin sheen of what from this distance looked like frost, opaque but glittering. And behind and around the cars Ellie could see other shapes moving.

The shapes looked like they might have been human once, or as if they were some fledgling attempt at being human that had gone terribly wrong. And they were white. Not "don't know how to season their chicken" white; not "don't ever forget your sunscreen" white. No: white like a bone bleached in decades of noonday sun. White as if someone had pulled a skein of damp cotton over their bodies and pulled it skintight. What might have been bright eyes, a pink mouth, were now drained of color, drained of life, and they moved as if someone had forgotten to give them eyes, or had maybe taken them, and they could only stumble, their hands reaching unseeing into the air.

Then one of them began to quicken its steps. Then two more. Moving faster now, their heads cocked every which way, fumbling along the cars, their hands grasping through smashed windows, open and shut, open and shut. They reminded her of a game she'd played when she had to take care of her cousins, three of them all younger than ten, and she'd toss all of their toys into a shopping bag and make them close their eyes, and she'd hide the toys in every corner of the yard. Blindfolded, one by one, they'd stumble around the yard grasping and feeling for the sharp bits of plastic, the soft faces of yarn, and she'd call out, "Warmer ... colder ... warmer ... hot!" while the other two watched, knowing theirs would come next. This, now, was how these pale things looked to her, shuffling faster and faster now as if something were pulling them towards a target their white eyes couldn't see, that she herself couldn't see.

And then she could.

Somewhere in the knot of frosted metal and wide open doors was a tiny lime-green sedan, and she could see a shape huddled inside, clothed in blue and yellow and wearing what looked like a head of long black hair. The frost at the window thickened, from what must have been a living human's breath. She imagined the chattering teeth, the clumsy hands stabbing at a useless phone, just as she'd been doing only a few minutes before. And now more of the pale figures turned their blind heads, and then she watched as they began flocking to the green car, their stumbling steps no less clumsy but quicker all the same. There might have been a voice calling in their ears: "Warmer, warmer, warmer, hot!"

"Look out!" Ellie screamed, as if the person could somehow hear her from so far away, and Terry clapped a hand over Ellie's mouth, but her other hand reached for Ellie's and they both whimpered without sound as the sedan's door snapped open and the shape bolted out and away from the swarm of white.

The shape was a human, deep brown skin like Ellie's and long black hair under a yellow hat, feet flying towards an escape. But the white shapes were coming from all directions, their grasping arms tangling and their pale bodies shoving each other aside. Ellie caught what must have been a pair of terrified eyes and then the jumble of white bodies squeezed themselves around their victim, and when they were done and shuffled along, the body thudded against the car's hood, the brown skin now covered in a layer of frost.

"That's what they did to her. To my partner. Diane. She was walking up there." And Terry's shaking chin stabbed at the bridge. "She was looking for a call box and she was almost to the bridge and they got her. Like that poor kid in the hat."

And then Ellie swung open the door and fell out onto the ground, retching her nearly empty stomach onto the asphalt. No way out of here, nowhere to go, and the white things were coming from two directions now, from the bridge and from the far end of the road where it dumped out into the cheap housing the City had shoved the poor in for decades. A lot of protection those rattling windows and thin walls must have been.

"You could run, Ellie. You're young. You might be able to outrun them."

Ellie stared at this woman, her mouth puckered with grief, the slightly gnarled hands that had brought warmth and comfort, those eyes that had never once judged. She shook her head and reached into the car and wrapped the red sleeping bag around Terry's shoulders, pulling it tight.

Just like always, what saved Ellie in that moment was nothing to do with her own choices, but pure, dumb luck. Barreling down the road from the bridge was a rust-colored hatchback that looked older than Ellie herself, swerving to avoid the white shapes stumbling in its direction. The driver took the turn way too fast and then overcorrected, and as the car fishtailed she could see a face flushed red, a mouth contorted in terror. And then the hatchback smashed into the front of the closed convenience store. The driver flapped once, twice, three times against the steering wheel, and then red began spreading over the thin white hair and along the arms. And in the space of three or four breaths, flames began licking their way up the car from the engine block.

Like moths, like lemmings, every white creature in sight began streaming towards the flames, and they did not stop themselves. They tossed themselves into the fire as it grew and consumed the car, and as the blanched bodies hit the flames what rose into the air was a plume of white steam.

So this was what those things were? A ferocious craving for warmth, an insatiable need that destroyed anything they touched, a hunger that was their own destruction? Like the owner of the Red Crow Saloon, the handsy one, a man who if he'd been surrounded by a mountain of white would have just kept sniffing until his heart stopped. Pale husks, these things were, without thought, without sight, and, maybe even, without sound. She threw one of the beer cans at the stragglers, the few still stumbling their way to the flames. No reaction, not even when she opened her mouth and screamed, "Hey! Whiteys!" in their direction. They just pulled themselves into the heat that consumed them, that turned them into steam in the night air.

"Ellie. Why weren't you scared?" Terry asked. Ellie felt for the fear that she knew was supposed to be somewhere inside but found nothing. Only a craving to see more of those things burn.

"I've never been good at self-preservation."

All around them—the skyline of San Francisco, the ugly towers in Emeryville, the hills surrounding the Bay—the lights were nearly gone. A few street lights blinked off and on, and what looked to be headlights slashed through the dark. Had those things broken their way through PG&E substations, drawn by the heat? Just like they must have done with the cell phone towers, and who knew what else. And it was so quiet. No squealing of ambulances, no thundering helicopters, no shouts from a megaphone ushering everyone to safety. Nothing but the white bodies shuffling in the distance and their victims draped along the bridge.

"How many people are dead?" She must have said this out loud, because Terry answered.

"So many. So many. And they got us first, didn't they? The ones sleeping in tents, in cars, the ones who had to be on the bridge at two in the morning." The truth of it stung. Thick walls, layers of fences, panic rooms: The rich would be fine, at least holding out longer than anyone else. The way it always was. In response Ellie slipped her lighter from her pocket and it snapped into flame.

"What are you going to do, Ellie—set the whole world on fire?"

"No. Just enough to draw them in. As many as possible."

"And then what? How do you even know that's going to work?"

"I don't. It's funny; I remember my mom telling me so many times that I needed to learn the difference between brave and foolish. I never really did. Guess that might be a good thing now." And she extended a hand to the shivering woman next to her, this stranger who was the closest thing Ellie had to a friend.

Terry glanced at the offered hand, shook her head.

"Ellie ... I can't. Did you know Diane was all I had left? No matter what I did or how low and mean I got, she still loved me. She could have left me more than once, maybe should have.

But she always said she saw our future"—and here Terry's voice grew thick—"And in it, we were together."

Against the wall the flames were beginning to die. Ellie tried to imagine what that kind of love must have been like. How long had it been since she'd known anything like that? If you didn't count family, maybe not ever. There was barely even anyone out there for Ellie to grieve. Except maybe most of the world.

"I'm not good at this stuff. You know, comforting people. But I do know Diane loved you so much she gave her life for you. You loved her, didn't you?"

"Of course I did." There was something in Terry's voice now, like a spark sputtering and trying to catch. Ellie could see white shapes flickering at the edge of her vision, on the eastern side of the bridge.

"Well, do you think she'd want you giving up and dying in an empty parking lot?"

Terry looked up, and now the spark was in her eyes, a flash of anger. Ellie didn't care if some of it was directed at her. She was used to that.

"Look, those things took her from you and I'm going to destroy them. As many as I can. And if you come with me, I can get more of them." Ellie leaned in to retie the loose flaps of Terry's hat, the rust-orange wool reminding her of coals waiting to bloom into flame.

"Listen—would you rather spend your last hours on earth crying? Or mad? Which would Diane choose?"

And now Ellie could see the light behind those damp eyes, and Terry stood, her trembling jaw setting itself tight. Terry shuffled to her car, and when she came back she was carrying two cans of jellied camp-stove fuel. And a lighter, a Zippo, its side engraved with the word "Diane."

"Rage." And in Terry's voice Ellie could hear the fuel igniting, the pale things hissing away into steam.

Ellie loaded up their backpacks: Terry's water bottles, some beef jerky and dried fruit, the cans of fuel. She tied double knots in Terry's shoes and they started along the road to the bridge, where the white things were trickling in for real now, from the east side of the span. Ellie took a swig of water and started singing the opening bars of "Welcome to the Jungle," and against the sky they could see the first streaks of dawn.

Content Warnings

- "Lips Like Sugar": workplace sexual harassment.

- "A Kiss to Build a Dream On": homophobia, references to police brutality.

- "The Nightmare Box": involuntary confinement, death by fire, references to child death, description of harm to children.

- "Will They Disappear": child abuse, neglect, and corporal punishment, more specifically a white family abusing adopted children of color, including three Black children.

- "Huitzol and the Rope of Thorns": references to police brutality.

- "The Road out of Nowhere": references to police brutality, racist language.

- "The Teachers' Association": gun violence, reference to child death.

- "The Weight of It": references to dog being harmed.

- "Red Brick": description of violence by law enforcement, racist language.

- "Someone Else's to Destroy": references to police brutality, racist language.

- "The Unburied": N/A.

- "Hot and Cold": N/A.

Acknowledgements

A book has a thousand tiny little midwives, and in this section I'm going to try and acknowledge as many as I can, with the creeping fear that I'm going to leave someone out somehow. I also know that there's no way I'm going to be able to express what your help meant to me. That said, I'm going to try. So:

As always, to my family, who've been supporting my writing in so many ways since I was writing it in crayon. And thank you for letting me borrow bits and pieces of you to weave into my characters, and into the stories themselves. A mi papá, por estar siempre tan orgulloso de mí. To Bree and Christopher and Francisco and Micah, who in very different ways kept feeding my desire to write and my fascination with the stories I longed to tell.

I owe a huge debt to the San Francisco Writers Workshop, where I brought every single story in this book. To my fellow writers, Silk Jazmyne Hindus, Tenaja Jordan, LP Kindred, Lindsay King-Miller, Mitch Lopes da Silva, Mara Olivas, T.K. Rex, Eric Raglin, Aurelius Raines, Zach Rosenberg, Peregrin Sánchez, and Gordon B. White, who read and commented on drafts, and drafts, and drafts. Thank you so incredibly much. (Huitzol is especially grateful to Gordon for helping me to untangle the threads of his story, so that Huitzol could see the light of day.) I don't know how writers used to make it without beta readers—maybe they didn't?—but I know I never would.

Speaking of Huitzol: George Galvis, who works with formerly incarcerated people, was seriously generous with his time in helping me gain perspective for the character of Roberto Salas. (For Roberto's life, I also took elements from the lives of real-life people who were killed by the police, including Sean Monterrosa and Alex Nieto. I encourage readers to look up their stories.)

Alex Lantsberg read a draft of "The Unburied" to help me understand some elements of construction sites, and Rudy Gonzales was very helpful in answering my questions about the same. NJ Gallegos helped me with a gruesome little medical detail for a story I won't identify, to avoid even the possibility of spoilers. I also got to spend a nerdily wonderful afternoon at the Oakland History Room at the Oakland Public Library, looking up maps and texts about the Chochenyo Ohlone, as background for "The Unburied." The Bay Area Lesbian Archives (and its late founder, Lenn Keller) were such helpful sources. Thank you. All of you. As always, any errors or misunderstandings are my own. And libraries, historians, archivists: You are some of the coolest people in the world.

And so are all my horror folks. And so are you, the person reading this. Thank you for picking up this collection. I hope you enjoyed the ride.

Publication History

- "Lips Like Sugar": published in *Luna Station Quarterly* (September 2023)

- "A Kiss to Build a Dream on": published in *Tree and Stone Magazine* (May 2023)

- "The Teachers' Association": published in *Bitter Apples* by Cursed Morsels Press (April 2023)

- "Red Brick": published in *Antifa Splatterpunk* by Cursed Morsels Press (January 2022)

- "Someone Else's to Destroy": published in *The Acentos Review* (May 2019)

- "The Unburied": published in *It Was All A Dream: An Anthology of Bad Horror Tropes Done Right Volume 2* by Hungry Shadows Press (March 2024)

About the Author

Cynthia Gómez (she/her) is a writer and researcher. She writes horror and other types of speculative fiction, set primarily in Oakland, where she makes her home. She loves to write dark and frightening things while cuddling with her shadow, aka her adorable little dog. Her work has appeared in *Fantasy Magazine*, *Strange Horizons*, *Tree and Stone*, and numerous anthologies. Her novelette, "The Shivering World," appeared in *Split Scream, Volume Two*, published by Tenebrous Press. *The Nightmare Box and Other Stories* is her first collection. You can find more of her work at cynthiasaysboo.wordpress.com.

Other Books from Cursed Morsels Press

Why Didn't You Just Leave

It's the question asked of any story about a haunting: *why didn't you just leave?* But if accounts of people who have stayed in haunted houses are any indication … it's never that simple.

In this book, you'll find twenty-two all-new stories about the reasons people *don't* leave scary situations—parents who stay in haunted houses to protect their children, convicts who literally can't leave their prison, retail workers who need a paycheck even if it's from a haunted workplace, trauma survivors suffering from agoraphobia, and more.

Featuring Shauntae Ball, I.S. Belle, Die Booth, Max Booth III, Christa Carmen, Raquel Castro, Alberto Chimal, Gabe Converse, Lyndsey Croal, Victoria Dalpe, Alexis DuBon, Corey Farrenkopf, Cassandra Khaw, Joe Koch, E.M. Linden, Steve Loiaconi, R. Diego Martinez, J.A.W. McCarthy, Suzan Palumbo, Tonia Ransom, Rhiannon Rasmussen, and Eden Royce. With illustrations by Luke Spooner, Yves Tourigny, and Yornelys Zambrano.

No Trouble at All

Politeness is the glue that holds society together. We are all expected to do our part—a pressure ripe with horror. Rotten, even. Whether we adhere to this contract or defy it, there are consequences. These fifteen stories respond to promises made for us, promises of compliance that cost too much to keep.

Featuring Nadia Bulkin, Shenoa Carroll-Bradd, Ariel Marken Jack, Gwendolyn Kiste, Avra Margariti, J.A.W. McCarthy, R.L Meza, Marisca Pichette, J. Rohr, Simone le Roux, Angela Sylvaine, Nadine Aurora Tabing, Sara Tantlinger, D. Matthew Urban, and Gordon B. White.

Bitter Apples

Cursed Morsels Press presents tales of teacher horror from Corey Farrenkopf, Emma E. Murray, Cynthia Gómez, Christi Nogle, D. Matthew Urban, Eric Raglin, and Aurelius Raines II. These writers have worked in the profession, and while their stories are fictional, the darkness they explore is all too real.

In *Bitter Apples*, you'll find students' ghosts haunting classrooms, desperate teachers joining cults, zombies plaguing underfunded schools, and more. The institution of education is rotting. How will we survive its horrors?

Shredded: A Sports and Fitness Body Horror Anthology

Reader beware! This sports and fitness body horror anthology is dangerous. Side effects include monstrous steroid transformation, concussion-induced madness, possession by jock ghost, death by yoga cult, and more. Read with caution!

Featuring seventeen reps of terror by Nikki R. Leigh, Tim Meyer, Brandon Applegate, Red Lagoe, Caias Ward, RW DeFaoite, Mae Murray, D. Matthew Urban, Charles Austin Muir, Joe Koch, Michael Tichy, Rien Gray, Robbie Burkhart, Eric Raglin, Matthew Pritt, Madeleine Sardina, Alexis DuBon, and J.A.W. McCarthy.

Antifa Splatterpunk

Fascism didn't die in 1945. Its grave was only temporary. Rising again, this undead ideology shambles into the present, gathering power and spreading destruction wherever it goes.

This monster stalks the pages of *Antifa Splatterpunk*, in which sixteen horror writers explore fascism's many terrors: police wielding strange bioweapons against the public, white supremacists annihilating their enemies through dark magic, and TV personalities vilifying all who defy the rising fascist tide.

But these stories are resistance: Nazi-killing demons, Confederate-slaying witches, and everyday people punching fascists in the teeth. Among the gore is a glimmer of hope that one day this monster will return to its grave and never rise again.

Forthcoming Cursed Morsels Releases

Lupus in Fabula, a horror and Weird fiction collection by Briar Ripley Page. Coming winter 2025.

Shaky Pictures of Vanished Faces, a horror and Weird fiction collection by D. Matthew Urban. Coming spring 2025.